MALIBU DREAMING

As the pain in her foot lessened, she became aware of how effortlessly he carried her across the sand; she felt like a feather in his arms. She was able to smell his lime cologne and feel his warm skin next to hers.

She had no choice but to put her arms around his neck, and, when she did, she became aware of the heavy thudding of her heart. He must have heard it, too. The feeling of his bare skin touching hers filled her with undeniable longing, far offsetting any pain.

She must have been dreaming it. It couldn't be true. For here she was gathered in Rob's arms, the sun sinking behind them, on the way to his beachside hideaway!

LOVESONG

Paula Williams

PAGEANT BOOKS

PAGEANT BOOKS
225 Park Avenue South
New York, New York 10003

PAGEANT and colophon are trademarks of the|publisher

Cover artwork by Ted Sizemore

Printed in the U.S.A.

First Pageant Books printing: July, 1988

10 9 8 7 6 5 4 3 2 1

To Bill,
for his unfailing love and support.
Thank you

LOVESONG

Chapter One
❖ ❖ ❖

IT WAS HAPPENING AGAIN.

Every time Callie faced the spotlights, a tremendous lump formed in her throat.

Clutching the icy metal microphone, she felt as if there was no way she could sing a single note, much less an entire song. Her palms would sweat, her hands would shake, and her heart would keep time with the rhythm of the drums. Except, unlike the drums, she was sure her heart would burst at any second.

And then when it seemed her body couldn't stand the tension a moment longer, a miracle would occur. The first note would leave her mouth; then the first few lines; and magically it would all come together. The lump in her throat would disappear; her palms would no longer be sweaty; and instead of a furiously beating heart, a feeling of pure joy would overtake her. It was as if she had been born for that one moment alone.

Once she overcame the initial jolt of anxiety, the joy of performing would seep into every vein of her body. She surrendered totally to the music and sang out with her entire being. For Callie, the music became a living entity—a safe place where her exorbitant emotional energy could be channeled.

Now, with the spotlights glaring down on her, the cameras for the video aimed in her direction, and Sizzle, her band, backing her up, she felt at home.

> *Has gotta be real . . .*
> *Has gotta be real . . .*
> *The way that I feel,*
> *Has gotta be real.*

By the time she reached the final chorus, Callie was wailing the words. She was so caught up in the song's emotions that for the moment nothing existed except the marriage of her voice and the accompanying bass guitar, electric piano, drums, and cymbals.

The session was going beautifully, Callie thought triumphantly. This could be the best song the group had ever recorded, and perhaps soon Sizzle would be back on top.

As the last notes of the song faded away, she heard an unfamiliar voice call out. "No, no. That's not the way it's supposed to be. . . ."

The response was so unexpected, it caught her off guard. Stunned, she froze, spontaneously lowering her arms as the microphone fell to her side.

She looked out past the cameras, past the recording equipment, and beyond the familiar faces of the band's usual entourage, to a tall blond man approaching the stage.

Immediately Callie recognized him as Rob Matthews, the composer of "Has Gotta Be Real." Although she had never met him, she had seen his picture in *Songwriter Magazine* on several occasions. And she also noticed he looked much handsomer in person.

"No," Rob repeated vehemently, "no. That's not right. That's not the way it should go at all."

"What do you mean, that's not the way it should go," Callie shot back, surprised at his unexpected attack.

"There's no line, 'the way that I feel.' That's not the way I wrote the song."

"Oh, come on now," Callie retorted, her normal feistiness coming into play, "it's just naturally coming out that way. I can't imagine a little change like that would make any difference to anyone."

"It does make a difference . . . to me." His velvety voice was mellow yet firm.

Callie glanced quizzically from Rob to gray-haired Vic Wilson, her producer.

Vic was silent. Looking down from the stage once again, she caught Rob's eyes with her own. As she saw their look of set determination, she also couldn't help noticing their deep aquamarine color.

"Well, surely one can allow for a bit of artistic freedom in the interpretation of a song," Callie said to break the hushed tension.

"Adding an entire line hardly constitutes artistic freedom," he answered.

Rob held her eyes with his steady gaze. Callie wanted to respond to his accusation, but didn't know what she could say to change his mind. And besides, he shouldn't be putting her on the spot in front of all these people.

Before she had the chance, the drummer, Tom Walden, interrupted. "Hey, we're wasting time here. Let's get on with it already." Tom was never one to be particularly subtle or patient, and now he was clearly demonstrating his lack of both qualities.

Callie was usually quick to stand up for herself, but she realized that she had to remain flexible in order to get what she wanted. In this instance, what she wanted was to sing the song the way she had rehearsed it. While she definitely had taken some liberties with the lyrics, she never imagined that the composer would object. Nor had she anticipated Rob Matthews's appearance at the session.

They never should have agreed to do the song without first retaining complete artistic control she thought to herself. Songwriters were always overly sensitive. But Matthews was too well established to go along with such an arrangement. Sizzle wanted to record several of his songs, figuring that with his past record for hitting the top ten, they couldn't miss. And, Callie thought to herself, they really needed a new hit soon.

"Well, I have an idea," she said, forcing herself to remain calm. "Why don't we do 'You Made Me Hurt Myself' now, and maybe Rob and I could talk about this problem later. I'm sure we'll be able to come to a mutually acceptable agreement." She smiled at him tentatively.

"That's fine with me," Rob readily agreed. "I have some appointments this afternoon, and I could be back here at, let's say, seven."

"Yeah. Yeah. Why don't you two hack it out between you later," the drummer interjected, impatient to get on with the session.

"Good. Then it's settled," Vic concluded, relief spreading over his features. "Rob and Callie can work this thing out later. Let's get on with the rest of the session now."

Callie pursed her lips, nodding in compliance while pushing her blond wavy hair away from her face. Rob gave her a half smile, but she thought she detected a confident twinkle in his eye. Then without another word he was out the door.

Watching him leave, his lean athletic body moving smoothly as he disappeared from sight, Callie felt her own body tense in irritation. Why couldn't things run smoothly—just once! The silence that followed Rob's departure filled the room as Vic approached her.

"Goodness, Callie, I sure hope you can handle

this," Vic said nervously, running a hand through his thinning hair.

"I do too," she replied, her confidence quickly waning.

"If Electric doesn't renew our contract, we'll have very little studio time left. And you know how long it takes to redo a song."

"I know, Vic, but I think I can handle it."

Callie's reassuring words did not betray her own trepidation. Despite Sizzle's continued popularity, they had had only one hit single in the four years she had been with the group. Now they were under intense pressure because Electric, the record company, was threatening not to renew their contract. Without the promise of a hit record and video, they had very little chance of being picked up by any other label.

Callie sought to reassure Vic with more bravado than she actually felt. Since she had become involved with the band she had become stronger —able to manage a fearless front even when she was trembling inside. She had always been a good performer, letting people see only what she wanted to reveal. But becoming famous had forced her to mask her softer, more vulnerable side.

Otherwise, she thought to herself, she seemed to get stepped on. Joining Sizzle had been a hard decision for her. She had always wanted to be on stage, yet walking into an established group left little room for her individuality to shine through. Still, right now she was committed to making their latest album a success.

Filing away these disquieting thoughts, she resumed her place at the microphone. Once again, she threw herself into the song.

> *You made me hurt myself . . .*
> *You made me hurt myself . . .*

For the next three hours Callie threw herself into the recording of the next cut.

If only one of these songs comes through for us, Callie silently prayed, we'll be home free.

The band, as if sensing her thoughts, were at their best, blasting their hard-edged beat loudly enough to shake the studio. The group's name was well chosen. They emanated a vitality and charisma that came across like a bolt of lightning. There was no denying their star quality, nor that of Callie Stevens, their lead singer. Hopefully the release of the album *Sizzle Sizzles Over* would skyrocket all of them to the fame they deserved.

"Cut!" Vic called out as he rushed to the stage. "That was great! Just great!"

Callie gratefully accepted his zestful hug. She knew the session had gone well. She could always feel when she was in sync with the band and the music. Today had been particularly high-spirited.

"Okay, everyone," Vic announced, "we got that track laid down perfectly. Let's break for the day and continue tomorrow."

The members of the band and the recording crew quickly packed their equipment, congratulating one another on a job well done. Callie noticed Rob slip into the back of the long room, and with his presence, her previous irritation returned. Something about this man disturbed her. She took a deep, determined breath. Noting the time on the studio clock, she glanced at Rob, who was now standing but a few feet away from her. "Looks like you're right on time."

"I try to be. Punctuality is important to me."

"As is exact adherence to your lyrics, no doubt."

"I assume that's what I'm here to discuss."

"Right," Callie agreed. "Let me grab my things, and if you don't mind, we could run over to the Hamlet to get a bite to eat. I'm famished!"

"Sure, why not," Rob agreed amiably. "It's always easier to argue on a full stomach." He silently led the way out the door.

Once they were settled into a cozy booth at the popular local hangout, Rob seemed to want to break the ice. And he started the conversation on a lighter tone.

"You entertainers never cease to amaze me," Rob said as he stared at the menu. "You sometimes seem to exist on air alone."

"Well, don't you ever get so wrapped up in your work that you don't have time to eat?"

"Oh, sure. All the time. But I always manage to keep a bowl of fruit or something nearby."

Callie laughed to herself. *Figures he'd like something healthful like fruit.* As she looked at him across the table, it was as if she were seeing him for the first time. *Damn, he's attractive with his thick blond hair and deeply tanned face.* When the waitress arrived, Callie ordered a large order of well-done French fries and a glass of white wine.

As she smothered the potatoes with thick red catsup, Rob observed, "That's hardly a feast for someone who just proclaimed she was famished. No wonder you're so slim."

Callie felt her face redden. Despite her attempts to appear cool, she had always blushed easily. And besides, she wasn't here to exchange personal observations with this man.

Matter-of-factly Rob added, "Of course, that's hardly a nutritious meal you have there."

"Oh, so now you're going to criticize the way I eat as well as the way I sing your song. Don't tell me, I bet you're into sprouts and granola."

"As a matter of fact, I am," he responded, grinning.

Callie was taken aback by her own words. Why did this infuriating man make her so defensive? She'd better lighten up if she wanted to come to terms—her terms.

He paused and gazed directly into her eyes. For a moment she completely forgot why they were there. Then, breaking the silence, he stated, "Really, I don't mean to criticize the way you're doing the song. Quite the contrary. I like the way you do it; I just can't accept some of the changes you've made in the lyrics."

As he produced the lead sheet for "Has Gotta Be Real" from his briefcase, Callie couldn't help but notice his powerful shoulders beneath his soft tan cotton shirt. The first few buttons were undone, and she could see his golden suntan. *Mr. Healthy,* she silently labeled him.

Rob continued. "About the changes; to start

with, I'm sure you realize that the line you've added to the chorus does not exist in the lyric sheet."

To restrain her temper, she stared deeply into her pile of potatoes. "Well, I'm aware of that. It just somehow evolved. Everyone in the group thought it added to the song. It seemed so natural."

"I don't agree. I don't like it that way." Despite his opposition, his voice was calm as a lullaby, strongly contrasting to the strong definition of his Roman nose and his firmly formed full lips.

"But Rob, we already have a good take of it that way, and we're pressed for studio time. It's such a minor change."

"Since *you* think it's so minor, why can't you switch it back to the way it was written? It's not minor to me. I'm sorry about the studio time, but it's not just a question of that line. There're other places where there've been changes. For example, the band repeats the chorus an extra time in the opening, which throws the timing off entirely."

She saw his point. She even sympathized with his position. But her career and the future of Sizzle depended on the outcome of this argument. At the same time, she was uncomfortably aware of a growing attraction to this impossible man.

"Hey, are you listening to me?"

"Huh," Callie offered brilliantly.

"I said you make other changes as well. In the third verse it should be 'the touch of your skin.' You were singing 'the touching of skin.'"

"Oh, please! Don't tell me you're going to get that petty!"

She took a sip of her wine, hoping its effect would somehow prove soothing enough to allow to assume a calm countenance. She wasn't really offended, but the band didn't have enough time to go back and change everything they had practiced and recorded to this man's specifications.

"Look, I don't mean to sound picky. It's just that I put so much into these songs. I try to get them perfect. And while I occasionally expect some artistic variations, and I certainly admire and respect your singing ability—"

"Please, spare me the compliment."

Yet, despite her sarcasm, she was becoming aware that Rob Matthews was unlike the people she usually dealt with in the music business. He seemed genuinely honest and forthright. And she genuinely liked him for his sincerity.

Still, she couldn't help but argue. "But I think 'the touching of skin' sounds better than 'the touch of your skin.'"

"That's interesting," Rob mused, a sparkle appearing in his deep blue eyes, "because that's the way I had originally written the line."

Callie reflected for a moment. "Tell you what. How about if we compromise? I mean, since you had written it that way originally, what harm could there be in letting me make that change?"

Rob remained silent for a few moments as he steadily looked at Callie from across the table. His staring caused her to shudder involuntarily. Perhaps the white wine was having more of an effect than usual. No, there was definitely something about his cool demeanor that was having an impact. She usually was much better at masking her vulnerability. I must be overtired, she reasoned to herself.

Then the smile that had begun forming on his lips moments ago blossomed into a full-fledged grin. Callie felt her tension subsiding as she became aware of how wonderfully attractive he was and how, despite herself, her pulse suddenly was racing out of control. No one had made her feel quite like this before. She couldn't help but respond with a full smile, her defenses suddenly melting away.

"You're too much," he jibed, nodding his head. "Okay. I can agree to that compromise, but there's still the question of the final verse. It's supposed to be 'this feeling I feel,' not 'this feeling I know.' That *does* make a difference, you know."

For the first time that day, Callie became fully aware of the heavy exhaustion that weighed on her. Normally she wouldn't back down so easily. "Okay. Okay," she relented, "we'll do it your way. Somehow, we'll relearn the song and redo the take. Mind you, it's not going to be easy. . . ." And it's going to use up a lot of precious studio time, she added silently.

At that moment the waiter appeared with the check, placing it midway between them on the table. Suddenly their hands collided as they reached for it simultaneously. She became aware of the touch of his skin and caught a whiff of a subdued, crisp lime cologne. A scrumptious but uneasy stirring spread through her slim body.

Within seconds Rob pulled his hand away. An extremely awkward moment followed. Callie felt a mixture of confusion and indignation.

"Please, don't bother. It's on me."

"No. No. I'll get it," Callie insisted.

"Look, we don't need to argue about this as well," he persisted as he removed a bill from his wallet, tossed it on the table, and took her coat, offering to help her into it.

She became aware of his body so near hers, and the rekindled sensations were unsettling. She pulled away, insisting, "Really, it's not necessary. I don't need any help."

"I don't mind at all," Rob responded, "but then, I guess you successful women sometimes resent such things."

"Oh, so now you think I'm Gloria Steinem just because I want to put on my own jacket."

"It seems to me that now you're the one who's jumping to conclusions," he said, a somewhat mischievous smile forming on his boldly handsome face.

She had to laugh in response, appreciating the silliness of her overreaction.

As they left the restaurant together, she felt dwarfed by his towering presence. He really was extremely good-looking, she said to herself.

"I hope you don't consider my offering to walk you to your car out of line," Rob said as they exited into the quickly escaping daylight, "but this isn't the safest neighborhood and you don't look like the type who has a black belt in karate."

"Oh, really. What does that type look like?" Callie asked, her dark eyes flashing.

"Hey, hey. How about calling a truce for the day," Rob said, his tone light.

The warm look in his eyes set her heart to racing again. "Sure," she said, laughing, and returned his smile.

As they made their way back to her sports car, Callie joked. "Hey, why are you walking so fast? This isn't the Boston Marathon."

"Sorry, it's just that I'm running a bit late. I have a dinner date."

"Oh, so you are stepping out tonight." She had wondered why he had ordered only spearmint tea at the restaurant, and she suddenly felt vaguely disappointed.

"If you must know, it's with a producer about scoring the sound track for a film."

She felt herself redden at her last remark. Why had the thought of him having a dinner date make her jealous? What was it about this man that set her off so easily? There was no doubt about it—Rob Matthews was pushing all the right buttons, and not just the ones in her head.

"Well, have a good meeting," she awkwardly offered as she stooped into her fire-engine-red Mercedes. Then, revving the engine, she sped away.

Chapter Two

❖❖❖

How DID IT go last night with Rob Matthews?" Vic asked nervously as soon as Callie arrived at the studio the next morning.

"It went fine. Just fine," Callie replied, as she walked to her microphone, and picked up some music.

"Does that mean that we don't have to redo 'Has Gotta be Real'?"

"Not exactly," Callie said hesitantly. "We compromised, but we're still going to have to make a few changes."

"Oh, that'll set us back, but I hear Matthews can be that way—really pigheaded. The problem is with studio time so limited, it's really going to be tight."

"Yes. I know. So Electric still hasn't made a move to renew our contract yet, huh?"

"Right. Looks like we're just going to have to look for another label, but I'll tell you, Callie, a lot is resting on this and we're not going to be able to reschedule studio time once the contract expires."

"Don't worry, I've already started relearning the song."

At that moment Ken Peterson, her lanky, bearded, keyboard player who had been setting up his music approached.

"Did I hear what I think I heard?" Ken inquired. "We're going to have to do another take on 'Has Gotta Be Real'?"

"Sorry 'bout that, Ken." Callie shrugged her

shoulders. She felt bad that she hadn't been able to talk Rob into changing his mind. But then, she already sensed that he was a man who stuck to his principles.

"Don't worry about it, kid," Ken offered. "Somehow we'll work it in."

"I sure hope so." Callie appreciated Ken's understanding but doubted if the other members of the group, especially Tom Walden would respond as calmly. Then, looking back in Vic's direction, she added, "I should be ready in a few days."

"Good. Then we'll continue with 'Class Reunion' today. I assume we haven't made any changes in that."

"No, but Rob's not going to be here again, is he?"

"I don't know. He may be. He has every right to show up when we're doing his songs."

"Oh, great. Just what we need. More complications." It was Tom this time, displaying his usual impatience.

"Don't worry, there won't be any more complications. Everything's under control," Callie said.

Everything, she reminded herself, except the way her heart raced whenever Rob was near. She hoped he didn't show up. And yet a part of her secretly wished that he would. There was no way she could deny it—she was attracted to his bronzed good looks and quiet strength.

This was no time for her to get entangled in a romance, especially since the band's future was up in the air. No, this was the time to put all her energy into Sizzle's album and videotape. Then

she had to prepare for their upcoming winter
tour.

"Hey, you won't believe what I just found."
Lynne Brynes burst in the studio followed by her
husband, Guy. Lynne played electric guitar for
Sizzle, while Guy was on bass. Waving a copy of
Starscoop Magazine, she yelled, "Look at this pic-
ture of Callie on the cover!"

Callie glanced at the glossy cover, which was
composed of a montage of couples including her
and Nick, with the headline, "Twosomes in the
Stars." She would never get over the thrill of seeing her picture on the cover of a magazine. As she
drank in her image, blond curls falling wildly to
her shoulders, bright smile lighting up her dark,
glistening eyes, she recalled the excitement of being seen with Nick and all the exposure it had
brought her.

"Oh, are they behind the times," Callie said jok-
ingly.

"Well, it's darn good publicity for the band,"
Guy announced. "Lynne and I sure didn't make
the covers when we tied the knot."

"Well, at that point we still hadn't hit the charts
with 'Razor's Edge,' " Callie reminded him.

"Let's face it," Lynne sighed, "even if it had, the
two of us would never get this kind of publicity."

"I probably wouldn't either," Callie replied, "if
it weren't for Nick. He's the crowd stopper."

"Come on," Ken said, interrupting her reverie,
"you stop plenty of crowds."

"And she's going to stop even more," Vic interjected, "once this video is released and MTV starts

rotating it on a daily basis. Which brings us back to business . . ."

"No rest for the wicked, huh?" Callie teased, not wanting to dwell any longer on the subject of Nick Steward. Although the rest of the band did not know it, the "romance" between herself and Nick had been engineered by a publicist. In her real life, romance had been hard to come by.

For years she had believed that no man was trustworthy; her father had proven that to her when he deserted her and her mother. Perhaps because her mother had remarried a wonderful man and moved with him and his children to Florida, Callie still believed that she, too, might find the right man someday.

When she met Nick, "Razor's Edge" was on the charts, and they made a hot news item. But as the song slipped in its popularity, so did Nick's attention. His publicity manager probably found another rising star to link him with, Callie had often thought.

" 'Class Reunion,' take one," Callie heard the familiar voice announce as she took her place at the microphone.

There was something about this song she loved. A ballad about high school sweethearts reuniting after years of separation, its sincere yet sentimental tone touched upon an all-but-forgotten innocence.

> *Class reunion and you're standing there,*
> *With that look upon your face.*
> *Class reunion and I'm standing here,*

Memories time can't erase,
Class reunion, class re . . . uh . . . ah . . .

She saw Rob standing at the back of the studio and choked on the words. She'd been so involved in the song, she'd momentarily forgotten about the person who had written it.

"Cut! Callie." Vic approached her. "Are you all right?"

"Oh, I'm sorry. I just, I . . ." She couldn't possibly tell him the truth, that Rob's presence had made her lose her concentration. "I guess I lost my train of thought."

"And it was going so well," Vic informed her. "Oh, well, we'll do another take now. That is, if no one objects." Callie thought she heard a sarcastic edge to his voice.

Of course she knew he was referring to her. "No, I'm fine. Really."

She was fine, now that Rob had taken a seat in the far corner of the room, where she was unable to see him. Really, Callie thought to herself, I have to start concentrating on my work. Not Rob Matthews. This time she put even more emotion into the words she sang.

"Fantastic!" Vic announced when they finished. "That was fast! A lot easier than a video! We'll just have to have the background dubbed, and that should do it for the vocals on 'Class Reunion.' It sounded great. Let's take a break for a few minutes while the crew sets up for 'Stormy Dreams.'"

Ken Peterson had written the next song, and Callie suddenly felt uneasy when she realized that

Rob would have no reason to stick around. She so wanted to speak to him. Impulsively, she made her way in his direction, a surge of adrenaline running through her, causing her already swift pace to quicken.

"Hi, how'd you like the way we did 'Class Reunion'? I didn't change a thing."

A meaningful silence filled the space they shared as Rob steadily scrutinized her from where he sat.

"I liked it. Very much." His voice was soft and somewhat sullen as his eyes met hers, a misty gaze making them appear older than she remembered. While at first there had appeared to be a sadness in them, shortly a familiar gleam reappeared. His voice lightened as well. "In fact, I wouldn't change a single thing."

Callie had been so tense while he was talking that she couldn't refrain from laughing out loud.

"And I like it when you laugh," he added as he met her smile with his. Just being close to him made her want to reach out to touch him. She yearned to stroke his muscular arm and know the strength of his embrace. Only the bustling of the crew setting up for the next take jarred her once again into the reality of the moment.

"Seriously, though, I'm very happy with the way you sing the song. You put so much feeling into it. It takes me right back to the way I felt when I first wrote it."

Had those words been spoken by anyone else, Callie would have considered them merely a line. But she already knew that Rob said only things he meant. She was glad she had come over to talk to him.

"Well, I'm thrilled, because I love the song. It makes me think of high school proms and pink corsages. Really, it's so wonderfully touching."

Now it was Rob's turn to redden slightly, which caught Callie by surprise. How refreshing to find a man so sensitive that he wasn't afraid to reveal his feelings. Apparently the song held a lot of meaning for him. She couldn't help but wonder what it could be.

When he raised his head once again, she inquired softly, "I assume it was written for someone special."

"Yes, it was," Rob acknowledged, taking a long, deep sigh, and then meeting her gaze. "I wrote it for my wife. I should say my ex-wife. We were high school sweethearts and then met again at our ten-year reunion. We married two months later." He paused and lowered his head before continuing. "It took a while before I was ready to have someone record it."

Callie felt a twinge of jealousy at the mention of his ex-wife. She could tell from the song how much he must have cared for her at one time. What was she like? How long had they been together? Did he still love her?

Looking at her again, his eyes lighting up as they met hers, Rob added, "Now I'm glad I released it and that you're the one who's singing it."

Before she could say anything else, Vic's voice called out from across the room, "Okay, everyone, what d' ya say we go through a few trial runs of 'Stormy Dreams' before putting it down on tape?"

"I guess I'd better be going," Rob replied as he stood up from his chair.

"Oh, no, you don't have to leave." Callie was aware of the words involuntarily slipping from her. She didn't want him to go yet knew there was no reason for him to stay. No reason, that is, except that she wanted him near her.

The floundering moment that followed caused an unwelcome flush to redden her face as Rob diverted his eyes and replied, "Well, some other time, maybe. I really have to be going now."

Much to Callie's dismay, it appeared that there weren't to be other times. In the days to follow, although they recorded other songs Rob had written, he did not reappear in the studio.

She searched for his face in the crowd during the next few sessions, hoping he'd appear. She even began to find herself thinking of him at odd times when she wasn't in the studio and the chances of running into him were nearly nonexistent. She searched for him while stuck in a traffic jam on the Santa Monica Freeway; she sought him out among the diners at the outdoor café that was frequented by people in the entertainment business. And while he never appeared in person, he always seemed to appear in her mind.

One morning while reading the latest issue of *Songwriter Magazine,* Callie found an article about Rob accompanied by a picture. As she gazed dreamily at the black and white photo, it was the caption that caught her eye. "Two-time Grammy Award–winner Rob Matthews composes another sure-fire hit at his beach retreat at Paradise Cove in Malibu."

Inspiration struck. If he wouldn't come to her natural habitat, she would seek him out in his.

Chapter Three
❖ ❖ ❖

SUNSHINE STREAMED ON the soft sand that greeted Callie's bare feet with a welcomed warmth. After being cooped up in the studio for so long, she rejoiced in her well-earned day off. Though the sessions were going well, they were exhausting. Now Callie ran with carefree abandon along the beach.

Although it was already late September, she could feel the sun beating down upon her, its brilliant energy seeping into every pore of her body. She felt free. As free as the sea gulls who were diving in and out of her vision with such streamlined precision.

No doubt about it, there was something unique about Paradise Cove. It had a quality of light that gave it an ethereal dimension. The atmosphere mixed with the freshness of the sea breeze and mist coming off the waves was exhilarating. She inhaled its magical air with delight.

No wonder Rob had decided to live here. Only fifteen miles north of Los Angeles, it felt light-years away. A euphoric peacefulness overtook her as soon as she stepped foot upon the sandy beach.

She had planned to arrive earlier, but the previous evening's session had run into the wee hours of the morning. It was already midday as she began to search for Rob among the sun worshippers who dotted the sand. Not catching sight of him, she spread out her beach towel. She liberally applied suntan lotion to her skin, pale from so many hours in the studio.

The thought of her mission made her tremble. She had never so brazenly pursued a man before. Still, she wasn't one to turn easily from a challenge. Especially a challenge as desirable as Rob Matthews.

The sun's rays felt comforting on her skin. That, combined with the roar of the waves crashing against the shore, calmed her. It was so luxurious to bask there lazily, with her large straw beach hat covering her face.

She couldn't be certain that Rob would even make an appearance, but judging from his deeply bronzed skin, she ventured it would be a good bet. However, what she hadn't anticipated was that the calm setting coupled with her exhaustion would lead her to drift into a lazy midday slumber. Startled, she awoke some hours later unaware of how long she'd been napping.

Annoyed at herself for possibly missing one of her only chances to see Rob again, she stared into the waves. Suddenly she realized a familiarly graceful yet muscular form was jogging in the distance. She was sure that it was Rob.

She watched him, shielding her eyes with her hands as he ran to the rock jetty and then turned around and started back in the opposite direction.

Gathering her courage, Callie took a deep breath, sprang to her feet, and made her way to him.

It was immediately apparent that he was totally involved in his exercise. When she called out his name, she could tell she had taken him by surprise.

"Callie Stevens! What are you doing here?"

"The same thing you are—enjoying the beach!"

His mere presence raised her already heightened spirits. She couldn't take her eyes off him as he continued to jog in place, generating a robust energy. He looked even better than she had recalled in her fantasies.

"But this is so far from L.A.!"

"It's not really that far. Besides, I like it here. I haven't been recognized by one person." She didn't bother to add that she had fallen asleep on the beach with a hat over her head so that even her own mother wouldn't have recognized her. "And this is much nicer than any of the beaches that are closer to the city. It's so special."

"Yes. It really is, isn't it?"

She felt like adding, "So are you," but held herself back, returning his full smile instead. Automatically her body had begun to shift slightly from side to side, keeping rhythm with his continuous movement, and she was beginning to feel as if she were at sea on a rocking boat.

They remained silent for a moment, the nearby waves occasionally tickling her toes as they foamed under her feet. She was mesmerized by the sight of his nearly naked body. Her eyes lingered longingly on his fine sun-bleached hair which blended into his well-formed, golden chest and then tapered down to his taut, muscular hips. Being this close to him, and so scantily attired, something long dormant within her surfaced. Once again, as she had in the studio days ago, she longed to reach out and touch him.

Finally, almost awkwardly, he broke the silence. "Well, I'd really like to talk, but I'm in the middle of my workout, and I can't stop right now. Maybe when I finish I can join you."

Now that she had found him, clad only in deep blue running shorts that nearly matched his eyes, she had no intention of letting him get away, not even for a minute.

"No need to stop. How about if I just jog along with you? I could use some exercise myself."

He appraised her skeptically. "Are you sure?"

"Sure. Why not?" Heck, she thought to herself, she'd show him. She might not be an Olympic runner, but how difficult could a little jogging be? After all, anyone could run.

"All right then, let's go. I do three or four miles daily, and I've already done two. So, let's see how we hold up."

She figured that one or two miles was nothing. No big deal. And at first it wasn't. She was too absorbed in just being near him, with his long, firm legs moving effortlessly next to hers. Their bodies were in sync, and she thought she detected a sensuous aura beginning to pulsate between them.

"How're you doing?" he called out.

"Just fine," she responded, trying not to breathe too loudly.

She sensed his eyes on her body. Although Callie never exercised, she was slim and in fairly good shape. Rob's flashing smile indicated that he approved of what he saw, and his affirming glance made her all the more eager to keep up her pace.

"This is fun. How far have we gone?"

"Nearly a quarter of a mile."

A quarter of a mile! She could have sworn they'd gone well over a half a mile by then. Her confidence quickly began to wane as her rib cage began to ache. Yet, she was determined to keep up with him, although it was obvious that he had slowed his own pace to accommodate her.

As their bodies kept moving in harmony, Callie tried in vain to suppress the weakening of her legs. Pushing herself to keep up her stride, her breath now coming in uneven spurts, she smiled gamely at Rob. Their eyes met for an instant.

"Are you sure you're all right?" Rob questioned with concern. "We could always stop."

The last thing she wanted was for him to stop his routine because of her. "Oh, no . . . I'm fine . . . just fine. . . ." She almost had to yell the words to be heard above the roaring of the sea.

Her breath was coming out in ragged spurts. The body she had so unashamedly flaunted a half mile or so ago was now covered with a decidedly unsexy film of sweat.

Still, she pushed herself. Gazing at the beauty surrounding her helped—the glaring sun beginning its descent in the azure blue sky, the sparse line of clouds along the horizon assuming a fuchsia hue, the waves surging against the shore, sometimes wetting her feet. But most of all she was aware of Rob's strong yet graceful body pumping beside her.

"My God . . . it's beautiful here. . . ."

"Yes, I've always thought so, I try to jog here nearly every day around this time. It helps me get in touch with myself. Helps keep things in perspective." As his hands gestured around him, his voice remained as even and smooth as the flowing sand.

She could almost visualize how the two of them looked against the sinking sun, and the image was so splendid it encouraged her to continue despite the pain she was feeling in every part of her body. She couldn't help but notice that Rob showed no sign of strain when he asked, "It seems so magical, don't you think?"

She was too winded to respond, so she simply nodded her head.

Suddenly she felt a sharp, jarring pain as her foot hit the sand awkwardly, forcing her to halt.

"Oh!" she cried out in surprise.

Gazing down at the ground below her, she saw blood on the bottom of her foot.

Instantly, Rob took in the situation. "Oh, Callie! Are you all right?"

"I don't know," she gasped, catching sight of the broken piece of glass responsible for her cut foot.

The sight of blood always made her weak, and this time was no exception. She fell to the ground, Rob quickly dropping down beside her.

"Let me look at the cut," his voice commanded, taking charge. "First, let's wash it off in the ocean. The saltwater should be good for it."

Perhaps the saltwater was good for it, but Callie couldn't help crying out as it stung her foot. "Ouch," she groaned, "it really hurts."

"I feel terrible! I never should have let you jog barefooted. It's all my fault."

"Oh, no, please, don't say that, Rob. It was foolish of me. I should have watched where I was going."

"Darn it! It seems rather deep," Rob observed, his face tensed in concern. "The lifeguards are off duty after Labor Day and I'm sure no one around here has a first aid kit. We'd better get you to my place, where we can wash and bandage it properly."

She almost felt like saying, "You just made me an offer I can't refuse." This wasn't the way she'd intended to get his attention, but she certainly wasn't going to complain about the sudden turn of events. She was helpless to do anything but comply with Rob's instructions. Making a temporary bandage out of a bandanna he had in his pocket, he swept her into his arms.

As the pain in her foot lessened, she became

aware of how effortlessly he carried her; she felt
like a feather in his arms. She was able to smell
his lime cologne and feel his warm skin next to
hers. She had no choice but to put her arms
around his neck, and in doing so, she became
aware of the heavy thudding of her heart. It was
beating so loudly, she could have sworn that he
could hear it. The feeling of his bare skin touching hers filled her with an undeniable longing, far
offsetting any pain she had previously been feeling.

Her scheme was succeeding beyond her wildest
imagination. Here she was, gathered in Rob's
arms, the sun sinking behind them, on the way to
his beachside hideaway!

Chapter Four
❖ ❖ ❖

SHE CLUNG TO Rob's chest, her heart beating furiously all the while as he carried her into his
house. As she got her bearings in his living room,
she became aware of an overall feeling of serenity. A spectacular view of the shimmering ocean
dominated the room and was complemented by
the beige and subdued sea shades of the walls and
the furniture. A sliding glass door led to a deck,
but before Callie could comment on the view,

Rob placed her on a soft teal blue leather couch and placed a towel under her cut foot.

"Now, you just lie there; don't move an inch."

"Actually, I was planning on doing some calisthenics, you know, jumping jacks . . ."

"Very cute, Callie. Does pain always bring out your funny side?"

What Rob didn't know, of course, was that despite her bleeding foot, her spirits couldn't have been higher. Her impulsive search for Rob had proved fruitful, and there was no doubt in her mind that her injury had been well worth the effort. Now that he was just inches away from her, she felt herself being drawn to him. *If only he would lean over and take me in his arms,* Callie thought.

"Now this might sting." Rob's statement broke into her thoughts, jarring her into the present as he returned to the room with a first aid kit from which he took a small amber bottle and some balls of cotton.

Her body stiffened as he dabbed the Mercurochrome onto her cut and proceeded to apply pressure. A moment later he reached over and rubbed her leg consolingly. "There, there. It won't sting for long."

He was right, but the pain in her foot was replaced by a tingling sensation all over her body. She had been so intensely involved in her career for the past few years that until that moment she had forgotten the tantalizing rush a man's touch could bring on. Especially a man as desirable as Rob.

"I think the bleeding's stopped." His attention was obviously on other places. "I'll bandage it and you should be good as new."

He reached for the first aid kit that he had placed on the chrome and smoked glass coffee table next to them and took out a roll of gauze bandages. Her eyes followed the contour of his muscular arm down to his strong, firm fingers she yearned to feel on her body. Oh, how she longed for his touch. But he appeared unaware of anything other than nursing her injury.

Suddenly, a gray cat appeared in the room and pounced on the gauze. "Sagan—you monster! Always around when you're not wanted." Rob teased the small feline, which was anything but a monster. In fact, Sagan was a true beauty—long silky hair that was almost silver with the sun's rays on it, smart white markings on his paws and face, and gleaming chartreuse eyes.

Just then Sagan made another bold attempt at the sheer gauze, diverting Rob's attention and causing Callie to whisper any number of four-letter words under her breath.

"Now, leave that alone, you crazy creature." Rob lightly pushed him aside. However, Sagan was not to be deterred quite so easily. Within seconds he had sneaked around the back of the couch and lunged at the roll of bandages. Once again Rob shooed him away. This time he appeared to get the hint but decided to direct his curiosity in another direction—namely to his surprise guest, Callie.

Making his way in her direction, Sagan slyly

began to sniff at her fingertips. Callie hesitated. However, before she could say or do anything, Sagan took an unexpected leap, landing comfortably on her lap.

"He does have good taste, I'll give him that." Rob smiled at her.

"Really, Rob, he's lovely, but I'm extremely allergic to cats—good taste or not."

"Why didn't you say so right away? I know what that can be like, especially for singers. I'll get him out of here."

Leaning over, Rob extended his hands and tenderly coaxed Sagan out of Callie's lap.

"Come here, you handsome gray ball of fur. Unfortunately, this gorgeous lady is allergic to you."

His complimentary words made her blush, but this reaction was not nearly as intense as the stirrings that shot through her body as Rob's fingers accidentally touched the skin on her inner thighs when he gently retrieved Sagan. She sat helplessly mute on the couch as Rob removed his cat from the living room. She was still unable to utter a word as he completed bandaging her foot.

She longed to reach out to touch him, to run her fingers through his thick golden hair, to feel his strong body next to hers. Her desire to touch him far overpowered anything else, and his insistence on making small talk was beginning to frustrate her.

When he offered her a glass of wine, she readily accepted, hoping that would loosen him up. While he went to get the wine she began to plan her seduction. Surely he must feel the chemistry between them, she mused. Certainly such feelings could not be one-sided. But how could she lure his attention away from her injury and into her arms?

"I can't believe it," Rob said, coming up behind her. "Looks like this just isn't your day. Not only have you cut your foot, but you've managed to get the beginnings of a nasty sunburn as well. Haven't you heard about the miracles of sun block?" he teased.

"Oh, I couldn't find my good stuff, so I used regular lotion instead. Besides, maybe you're double-jointed, but I'm not," she jested, aware for the first time of the burning sensation on the areas of her backside that weren't covered by her bikini.

"Here. I'll pour you some wine, but we'd better get some aloe cream on that burn right away."

Besides the wine, Rob had brought out a wooden tray with an assortment of cheese, crackers, and sliced apples. His trusty bowl of fruit, Callie thought as she remembered their first encounter at the restaurant. How much had changed since that initial meeting. And yet nothing had changed, she reminded herself.

Or maybe it had. Rob allowed her merely a few sips of the refreshing white wine before he got the cream from the ever-ready first aid kit and turned her on her side. He kneeled on the floor beside her and began to apply the ointment to the burned areas of her upper back. As he did so, her senses began to whirl out of control. She was totally unaware of the raw sunburn, for the feeling of Rob's strong yet sensitive fingers were far more overpowering.

He moved slowly along her shoulder blades and down her back. His touch was strong yet soothing, and it felt as if his fingers were made to touch her skin. When he reached her midback at the point where the bow that held her bikini top together was tied, his fingers lingered for a moment. Briefly he removed his hands to apply more cream and resume his massage.

The more he massaged her, the less she was able to control the sensations that were exciting her.

"Does it hurt much?" he asked.

Flustered by his ministrations, Callie only managed to say, "No, no. It doesn't hurt."

"Well, I bet it will tomorrow," he responded, and continued applying the cream, now to the upper area of her thighs.

"I can't believe how soft your skin is," she heard him whisper. "And your legs . . ."

Not letting the moment slip away, she rolled over. Their eyes met, and just as she felt her heart was about to burst, his lips came down strongly upon hers. It was an urgent kiss, as if he, too, had been holding back all the while. She responded with uninhibited eagerness.

She could taste the delicious crisp wine as he parted her lips and thrust his tongue into her mouth. She pulled him even closer to her, their nearly naked bodies generating more heat than even the sunburn could give off. She felt her nipples harden against his massive chest and wished to be rid of the scanty top that kept her from him. As if he could read her mind, she felt his fingers begin to pull on the bow.

And then it happened. A shrill sound. The telephone! It rang so loudly, she jumped.

Oh, let it ring, please let it ring, Callie pleaded with her kisses searching out the hidden corners of his mouth. She dug her fingers into Rob's strong back as encouragement.

"Dammit! I almost forgot. I'm expecting a call— it's important. I've got to get that."

She wanted to cry out, "What could be more important than what we are doing?" Rob broke their embrace, jumped up, and ran for the telephone, which was at the far end of the room directly in front of the sliding glass door.

His body was silhouetted by the setting sun. Callie recalled the pressure of it upon her. Aware of conflicting emotions—blissful joy coupled with the feeling of abandonment, she watched him across the room. Once again she pondered—what could be so important to tear him away from her like that?

She had to eavesdrop. She had to know.

"So she gets that as well, huh?"

His question was followed by a long silence. Callie found herself drifting back to reality. Once again she was aware of her bandaged foot and stinging sunburn. But more than ever she was aware of the way she was feeling about Rob. The heated kiss had intensified her preexisting emotions. But now she was jealously wondering about the "she" Rob had referred to and what it was that "she" would get.

"Yes, I was aware of that." Rob's agitated voice broke the hush. "But it was just an oversight on our part."

Silence followed by "Yes, yes, I understand."

Callie didn't know what he understood, but she did know that the atmosphere had changed drastically. She sensed the depression of his present mood, which so radically contrasted with their thrilling embrace of moments ago.

Finally, she heard him say, "Well, thanks for taking care of this so quickly. I appreciate it, though I wish it had been better news."

When he hung up the receiver he paused a moment. The sun had almost entirely sunk into the horizon. His well-formed, lean body appeared shadowed against the backdrop.

"I'm sorry, but I had some unfinished business," Rob stated. His face was now drawn, and she was all too aware of his abrupt mood change. How she wished the telephone had not rung; how she longed to be back in Rob's embrace, his tongue thrusting inside her mouth sending waves of pleasure to her innermost being. But it was too late to wish for that now.

"Do you want to talk about it," she offered meekly.

"No, I really shouldn't burden you with my problems."

"It's not a burden," Callie offered.

Rob hesitated, appraising her for a moment, then said, "It's just that I thought it was all over. I

mean, my divorce was final over a year ago." He
was pacing the floor now. "But I had neglected to
list one of my songs in the settlement. It was
merely an oversight, but Gloria caught it. She actually accused me of trying to keep it from her,
which is ridiculous."

"I don't understand. What do your songs have
to do with her if you're divorced?"

"Plenty. Legally, she has a half interest in anything I wrote while we were married."

"You're kidding!"

"No, that's the way it is in California. You see,
this is a community property state, and my songs
are considered property."

Callie was incredulous. "But they're *your* songs
—they're works of art! I can't believe it."

Rob came over and sat by the edge of the
couch. He looked at her. "Actually, it's not entirely unreasonable. You see, Gloria supported me
while I was a struggling songwriter. It was her
career that allowed me to write. Ironically, it was
also her career that destroyed us. Her travel
agency mushroomed and became more and more
demanding. She was constantly on the road, and
that tore us apart."

A silence came between them. Callie mentally
thought of all the time Sizzle spent on the road,
and wondered if Rob was thinking the same
thing. He became sullen for a moment. Then,
nodding his head, he sighed. "It's probably just as
well the call interrupted us."

"How can you say such a thing?"

"You know how I can say that."

"But Rob, how can you deny what just happened?"

"I can't deny the chemistry, Callie, but look at us—we're as different as Beethoven and the Beatles. You're a fast-food addict, while I'm into health food. You're delightfully scattered, while I'm neat and orderly. Why, you're even allergic to my cat!"

"I can't believe my ears! How can you stand there and tell me that you didn't feel what I was feeling? How can you!"

"I don't want to discuss this anymore, Callie! I just don't. Here, let me help you gather your things and send you on your way home."

Callie sensed there was no point in arguing. Not now anyway. Rob, silent as he lent her a sweater for protection against the cool night temperature, drove her back to the beach parking lot to her car. She longed to reach out and touch him, but he seemed miles away from her.

As she headed home on the winding highway along the ocean, Callie felt a salty tear falling down her cheek. It was then she recalled Rob's warning that she would feel her sunburn in the morning. But as she blinked away the tears, she knew that wouldn't be the only thing that would be hurting her.

Chapter Five

❖ ❖ ❖

TAKE FIVE. 'Has Gotta Be Real,' " Vic announced.

Today things just weren't going Callie's way. Although the words to "Has Gotta Be Real" were ironically appropriate and she sang them with full emotion, the song just wasn't coming together. Perhaps if she could stop peering at the door, wishing it would open, hoping Rob would appear, the song would flow, but she couldn't and the session was extremely frustrating.

That's how the past few days had been. No matter how she tried, she couldn't get Rob off her mind. She even knew she was being silly, acting like a teenager again. But she just had never met anyone like him before. Since she had become a professional singer, she made few real friends. Yet her pride stopped her from calling and pleading with him. She assumed he'd be at the studio for the remake of the song. Why had he stayed away? He'd been there when they'd done his other songs. After all the difficulties with "Has Gotta Be Real," Vic had notified him of the session. But still there was no Rob in sight.

"No. No. No!"

Vic approached the stage, gesturing as if he were about to pull out what little remaining hair he had. "Callie, what's the problem? Is your foot still bothering you? Is your sunburn affecting your performance? Tell Uncle Victor what's the matter."

Of course it wasn't her foot or sunburn that was

bothering her, but she couldn't tell Vic her problem. This wasn't like her. She was a professional. She knew she must concentrate and throw herself into the song. But she just couldn't concentrate!

"Don't worry," she sighed as she pushed her hair away from her face, "I'll get it right this time."

"Good God, I sure hope so," Tom said, as he tapped idly on his drum.

"Okay. Let's take it again. 'Has Gotta Be Real.' Take six."

> *How long has it been?*
> *How long have we known?*
> *The touching of skin?*
> *The feeling within that's making us glow . . .*
> *As short as it's been,*
> *As long as I feel*
> *This feeling within*
> *Has gotta be real . . .*

There! She finished the entire song. And this time it was good—she could sense it.

"Finally!" Vic's voice echoed in relief.

Callie took a deep breath. She gazed around the studio. A hand was waving vigorously in her direction. For an instant she thought Rob might have entered while she had been singing his song. Disappointment soon overtook her. It was a female hand.

"Don't look so thrilled to see me," her dearest friend said sarcastically. "You told me I was welcome anytime, but now I wonder if you were serious."

"Don't be silly, Sharon! Of course I was." Callie gave Sharon an affectionate hug. "It's just that it's been a rough day."

"Well, if it's a bad time—"

"No. Not at all. In fact, we're due for a break. I know a place where we can talk," Callie said, adding in a whisper, "and I sure could use a shoulder to cry on."

Since she had become famous, there were so few people Callie could trust. So Sharon's appearance today was truly a blessing. Her friendly smile and easygoing manner would be a balm to her spirits. Maybe Sharon could answer her questions. Maybe she could tell her what to do.

Callie directed her friend to the same restaurant she had gone to with Rob the first time they had met. Being there somehow brought back that evening and its vivid memories. Why was she torturing herself like this, she silently pondered as they were seated at a table near the one she had sat at with Rob. At least it wasn't the same table, she consoled herself as she told Sharon about the recent developments at the beach house.

"Why, I'm surprised at you, Callie Stevens!" Sharon exclaimed after Callie recounted her dilemma. "Since when have you been one to shy away from a challenge!"

"But this isn't the same, Sharon. He's so different—he's special." Rob's image formed in her mind, bringing memories of the way her senses had come alive when he touched her, the way her

lips had turned to fire with his kiss, and the rushing sensation that had spread throughout her
body as he wrapped his arms around her.

"I can tell by the look on your face that he is,"
Sharon responded, a delighted twinkle in her
brown eyes. "I've never heard you react so
strongly to a man before. Perhaps this is the real
thing."

"But what good does it do me?" Callie la-
mented. "He doesn't want anything to do with
me. He thinks I'm like his ex-wife and that all I
care about is my career."

"Then you have to convince him otherwise.
Look, Callie, you've always gone after your
dreams. Remember when you tried out for Sizzle?
At first they didn't want someone as young as you,
but you persuaded them. And how about how
hard you worked on all those plays at school. No
part was ever too challenging for you. If you want
him, go after him."

"I don't know, Sharon. Lately Sizzle doesn't
seem like enough. It sure doesn't mean much
when I'm all alone late at night or when I wake
up in the morning to an empty house."

"That's one thing my house never is," Sharon
said wearily, but there was a smile on her face,
"empty. Not with Doug and the kids romping
around. Sometimes I feel like a little solitary
peace and quiet for a change."

"Yeah, like a few hours, huh? But you know
how much you'd miss them if you didn't have
them."

"You're right about that," Sharon confessed.

She fell silent for a few moments. When she continued, her voice was quieter, her tone pensive, "You know, Callie, I don't think I've ever heard you talk like this before. This guy is really having an effect on you."

"Yeah, but what difference does it make if he won't even see me?"

"Make it a point to see him," Sharon insisted. "Surely you can concoct a reason."

A reason. Something nonathletic this time. Suddenly, Callie sat up straight in her chair. Of course—the sweater! She would return the sweater he had lent her.

"Oh, Sharon, you're an angel to help me with this! I just can't thank you enough!"

"Please, Callie, after all you've done for me! For goodness' sake, you were the one who introduced Doug and me. The least I could do is listen when you need a friend."

"Yeah, but lately you're the one that's been giving me all the support. Sometimes I feel a little guilty."

"Then maybe I should refresh your memory a little." Sharon gave Callie a mischievous smile, her pixielike face lighting up. "Remember the time in high school when I lost my final math assignment and you stayed up half the night with me so that I could get it in on time?"

"Yes, I remember that, but math was always a snap for me. What about the time you helped me collect those horrid insects so I could pass biology?"

"Oh, my goodness, I remember those horrible things! What did you ever do with them?"

"I gave them to Cindy Rose when *she* had to have a project to pass biology."

"You're kidding! It's hard to believe the poor things lasted that long!"

"They didn't," Callie burst out, shaking with laughter at the memory.

Both women were nearly crying from laughter now. Callie was grateful her friend had stopped by and lifted her spirits.

"That's what friends are for," Sharon reminded her as they hugged. As Callie waved good-bye in front of the studio, she was already planning her strategy.

She could barely wait for the day's session to end, she was so keyed up with anticipation over seeing Rob again. However, when they finished the final take, Vic called her aside.

"Got a moment?"

"Ah, actually, I'm in a bit of a hurry."

"Big date, huh?" he beamed at her. "Well, then I won't keep you. I just wanted you to take a look at the itinerary for the upcoming West Coast tour. We can talk about it another time, but I'd like some feedback before finalizing the hotel reservations and all."

The West Coast tour was the last thing Callie wanted to deal with. It was too much of a reminder about the demands of her career—and of the barrier that was coming between her and Rob. She hastily took the folder, assuring Vic that she would give it some thought.

*   *   *

On her way home Callie debated whether she should call Rob or simply show up. As she gulped down some cold leftover pizza, she opted for the latter.

After a quick but steamy shower she rubbed silky lotion onto her skin. She sprayed expensive perfume liberally over her body, inhaling its rich fragrance with delight. She put on her newest red sundress, hoping Rob would notice the effort she had put into her appearance.

She applied makeup sparingly, for the sun had already given her a glowing color. Of course her shoulders and back were already peeling from their overexposure, but the thin, light material of her outfit covered the burned areas. The sight of the burn brought back the memory of Rob's hands on her body. She wondered if she would feel them again that night. The possibility brought on a tingle of anticipation that stayed with her even after she maneuvered her small sports car onto the Pacific Coast Highway.

But as she approached Paradise Cove and neared the turnoff to Rob's house, doubt began to creep in. Should she have called first? What if he weren't home, or worse, what if he were and was with another woman? Nervously clutching his soft wool sweater between her fingers, she reassured herself that she had made the right decision.

Callie heard the melodic sound of the piano as she approached Rob's front door. The tune was pleasing yet unfamiliar. She listened attentively, appreciating the flowing notes of the ballad. Then the playing stopped. Callie rang the bell and waited, her nerves tensed in anticipation.

It was too dark to decipher the expression on Rob's face when he answered the door, but she immediately sensed the strain in his voice despite his attempt at humor. "Callie! What a surprise! Don't tell me, you just happened to be in the neighborhood and decided to stop by."

"Not quite, but I thought you might want this back." She held the sweater out in his direction. She searched for a reaction in his eyes but was unable to see clearly in the dimly lit entrance.

"I'm impressed. You drove fifteen miles to return my sweater."

"Actually, I had planned to return it at today's session, but you didn't show." A white lie, but one she felt appropriate at the moment. "We did the remake of 'Has Gotta Be Real' today, you know."

"I know. Vic told me." She heard him sigh.

"Can I come in?"

"Sure. Sure. Suit yourself."

"I really thought you'd be there today," Callie said, attempting to make light conversation. She hoped to divert his attention, for her heart was beating out of control at the sight of him. As he towered over her, she felt more vunerable than ever and yearned to be grabbed up into his arms.

"Ordinarily, I would have been," Rob confessed. He paused. The way he looked at her made her tremble.

"We've got to talk," she blurted out, catching his eyes with her own.

The earnest look that met her gaze told her that she had made the right decision in driving out to see him. More than ever, the chemistry was undeniably there, filling the space they shared as it had the last time they had been together.

However, his next words weren't the ones she wanted to hear. "Callie, I know we do. But I don't know that I'm ready to talk yet. That's why I wasn't at the session today, and that's why I'm hesitant about inviting you in."

"I can't wait any longer," Callie implored. "You have no idea how it's been for me these past few days. I'm not going to play games with you, Rob. I can't."

"Nor do I want you to, Callie. But I don't know if I'm ready to talk about this."

Talking was not necessarily what Callie had in mind at that moment. Her body longed to feel the powerful strength of Rob's, and her senses yearned to be ignited as they had been a few nights before. She couldn't help it—he had that effect on her.

He must have sensed her longing, for he quickly averted his gaze and moved away from the arms she had spontaneously extended in his direction. The sharp silence that filled the room was fraught with unspoken desires.

Determined to alleviate the tension, and uncomfortable that she might be coming on too strong, Callie offered, "I liked what you were playing before."

"Did you really?"

"Very much so. Is it new?"

"As a matter of fact, it is."

"Could I hear it again?" she inquired out of genuine desire to hear the melody as well as the craving to spend more time alone with Rob.

"Sure, I'd be glad to play it for you, but I'm expecting someone soon."

Her heart sank. She wondered whom Rob could be expecting—undoubtedly a woman. Her disappointment must have shown, for Rob quickly added, "A singer is coming over to do a few demos for me."

I'll bet that's what she's going to do, Callie thought sarcastically. Why would he have her come over at night? As Rob led her to his studio, she attempted to check her misgivings, but they would not disappear quite so easily.

Rob's studio was located on the far end of the house. From the moment she stepped into it, she was enchanted. Imagine, being in the very room where he created the splendid tunes that had made him so famous.

An ebony grand piano dominated the space. There was no view or windows, undoubtedly to avoid the moisture that could affect the marvelous instrument and extensive recording equipment. One wall was entirely dominated by gold records and Grammy awards for songs he had written. Another wall had shelves loaded with record albums and tapes. A few straight-back chairs were scattered around.

Rob made his way to the piano, and Callie wasn't sure if she should join him at the bench or pull up a chair. She chose the latter, placing it behind Rob, where she could easily observe him.

As his fingers glided along the smooth ivory keys, Callie's apprehension began to fade. Something about the tune was reassuring. She became lost in its mellow flow. It made her want to put her arms around him. If only she had the nerve! But after his most recent rebuff, she feared she would only alienate him further.

When he completed the piece, he turned and looked at her with his eyebrows raised in question.

"That was beautiful," she said, honestly. "Just beautiful. Do you have words for it yet?"

"Oh, I'm working on them." Rob gave her a sly smile. "Perhaps I'll even ask for your advice."

Callie smiled. Things had obviously changed. Rob appeared relaxed, his previous defenses magically vanished.

But then he glanced at his watch, stood up from the piano bench, and announced, "Patty should be here any minute. In fact, she's late . . ."

Patty. So that was what his "singer" called herself! Callie could no longer restrain her emotions. "But Rob, we need to talk!"

"I know we do, Callie. But I need more time to think about things."

"Then maybe I should give you something to think about," Callie insisted. She walked over to him slowly, and seductively placed her lips on his. At first she sensed a resistance, but then as she dug her fingers into his back and began to explore his mouth with her tongue, he began to

LOVESONG 51

respond. Once again she felt the fire igniting between them. Time melted away so that all that remained was the pure sensation of the moment.

He kissed her back, drawing her closer in his arms. She felt his muscular body next to hers and felt tiny and secure in his embrace. She could feel the thick fullness of his hair as she ran her fingers through it. She longed to have him even closer, to be totally immersed in his embrace. Suddenly, he stiffened and pulled away from her.

"Listen, Callie, we've got to stop. There's a lot we need to discuss, but this isn't the right time."

"Okay, then, when?"

He looked at her, and she sensed the confusion in his eyes, but she couldn't leave without getting him to commit to a time. "How about Friday. Friday night?"

"Yes, sure. Friday night. I'll take you out to dinner. Get you something healthy for a change."

She appreciated his attempt to lighten things up, so she went along. "Yeah, sure. Maybe we could go to the zoo and join the rabbits. Get some carrots and cabbage."

"That isn't quite what I had in mind, but if you'd prefer the zoo to Geoffrey's—"

"Oh, no. Geoffrey's sounds fine to me."

She knew of the small but elegant Malibu restaurant. Since it was relatively unknown, they might be assured of the privacy they would need.

The ringing doorbell told Callie that Rob's singer had arrived. As they made their way to the door, she pursed her lips and shrugged. Might as well meet the competition, she conceded.

When Patty—at least seven months pregnant—
burst into the scene, Callie had to bite her lip to
hold back her laughter at her own foolish jealousy.

"I'm sorry I'm late, but I had trouble getting
Brucie to sleep. Jim just doesn't seem to be able
to—" And then she stopped, obviously becoming
aware of Callie's presence.

"Oh, my God. I didn't recognize you at first! Callie Stevens!"

"Patty Lorenzo, meet Callie Stevens." Rob introduced them, amused by Callie's obvious discomfort.

"I just love your work," Patty gushed. "I mean, I
don't know what to say. . . ."

"Well, from what I've heard of the demos you've
made for Rob, you could give me a run for my
money."

"Oh, no. I could never sing like that before a
live audience. That takes something special that
you have and I don't. Anyway, Jim and I prefer it
this way—making demos and singing occasional
backup. It works out better with a toddler at
home and another one well on the way." She gave
a grand but unnecessary gesture, indicating her
protruding belly, and then babbled on. "And
Rob's been so understanding, letting me come in
odd hours to do demos."

"Speaking of which," Rob interjected, "we have
work to do."

"I'd better be going." Callie shrugged.

"It's been so great meeting you," Patty reiter-
ated. "I can't tell you how much I admire you."

"Thanks," Callie returned, but couldn't help but wonder if Rob didn't admire a woman like Patty more—one devoted to her husband and children. The thought haunted her as she drove into the dark, misty night. Maybe that's what Rob wanted, a woman who would put her man before her career. But was that what she wanted to do? All she felt sure of at that moment was that she wanted Rob more than she had ever wanted any man.

Chapter Six
❖ ❖ ❖

TELL ME, CALLIE, why do you think the group hasn't hit the charts again since 'Razor's Edge'?" the woman asked, not wasting any time in getting right to the heart of the matter.

Inwardly Callie flinched. Interviewers rarely spared one's feelings. "It's often difficult to predict trends." Callie sighed. "And it's especially difficult to follow a smash hit with an equally exciting song. For a while we didn't have the right material, but now we do."

"So you think your upcoming album, *Sizzle Sizzles Over,* is going to put the group on top again?"

"Oh, yes!" Callie's voice rang out with confidence, concealing any doubts she might possess. She hoped her answer would prove true. It couldn't hurt to have a positive attitude. Camera bulbs were popping as she attempted to give off her most radiant smile.

"Could you tell the readers of *Rocking Stone* which songs you're most excited about?"

"I am personally excited about several of the tunes," Callie responded diplomatically, "but 'Has Gotta Be Real' and 'Class Reunion' are among my favorites." She smiled and reflected—the writer is pretty exciting too.

"What about Nick Steward?" The question stunned Callie, not so much its content, but because it was the photographer, rather than the interviewer who had shouted it across the room.

She hesitated. "Uhm, he's doing quite well, I believe."

"But I mean, what about the two of you?"

"You don't have to answer that if you prefer not to." The interviewer gave the bald, wiry photographer a disapproving look. "We're here to discuss your music, not your love life."

Callie was relieved to have the question dismissed. *Rocking Stone* was one of the most respectable publications in the music business, and although they occasionally printed gossipy items about various stars' love lives, she didn't want this interview drifting in that direction.

"Tell us about Sizzle's new video?"

"This is going to be a first for Sizzle because we plan to release it prior to the album. It features 'Has Gotta Be Real' and should be the most exciting video we've made yet."

"Rob Matthews wrote that, didn't he?" the interviewer asked. "And a number of other songs on the album, I believe."

"That's true. We're lucky to be doing his songs." Callie struggled to keep her voice neutral as a quiver of excitement overcame her at the very mention of Rob's name.

"What about the two of you? Any rockets being set off?"

She glared at the impertinent photographer, grateful that he had not taken a picture of her reaction to his statement. Damn these journalists. They got more acute every day.

"Scratch that question." The interviewer threw a dirty look at her colleague.

Simultaneously, Vic intervened. "Really, it's been a long day and the end of a long week. Callie must be exhausted. She needs some rest. I'd be happy to stay and answer any further questions you might have."

Callie appreciated Vic's thoughtfulness. The last thing she needed was the press to leak anything about her and Rob. Especially when things were so tenuous!

"That would be fine," the interviewer agreed.

"Just let me get a few more shots."

Despite his brazen behavior, Callie felt compelled to comply with the photographer's request. As the bulbs flashed, she took a deep breath and attempted to forget his rudeness. She concentrated on thinking about Rob instead, recalling his bronzed good looks, his muscular physique, and most of all, the feel of his firm lips upon hers. She reminisced about the way she felt in his arms and fantasized being in them once again. Undoubtedly, the memory must have brought a twinkle to her eyes. If only the ill-mannered photographer knew what was putting that gleam there.

After the aggravating yet necessary interview, thoughts of Rob remained. As she drove home through the rush-hour traffic she daydreamed about their dinner date that evening. What could she wear that would project the proper image? She wanted to look simple yet elegant, but these two adjectives hardly described the wardrobe of a rock and roll singer.

By the time she decided, a mountain of clothes were piled high upon her bed. She chose a sensational and somewhat clinging jersey dress in shades of pink and black. She complemented the outfit with a pair of soft, fashionable black leather boots and a striking ebony necklace with matching drop earrings. The look was stylish but understated. The lines showed off her figure while at the same time maintaining the look of simplicity she was striving to achieve.

"Sorry if I'm a little late," Rob apologized at the door. Callie glanced at her watch and noted that he was hardly three minutes late. "It was my sister's birthday, and we got carried away on the phone."

"Oh, I didn't know you had a sister."

"Two of them." Rob gave her a proud smile. "Clare's at school and Joan's still back home."

"Where's that?"

"Bellingham. Washington. It's on the coast, a bit north of Seattle."

"Seattle's a nice city. So green."

"Yes." Rob temporarily appeared to be far away, as if he were reminiscing about the past. "Green but wet. Southern California does have some things going for it."

They stepped out into the dry California night air and Callie couldn't help but catch his meaning. "Still, you must miss them."

"I do. But we're always on the phone and we get together as often as we can. That's one of the reasons I bought a house with three extra bedrooms —I keep two of them ready for them. But it's hard for them to get away. My father's a doctor and Clare's busy in school in San Francisco."

No wonder Rob was so solicitous of her, wanting her to eat healthy foods, Callie reflected as she slid into the smooth leather seat. Growing up with two younger sisters must have had an effect on him.

As they glided along the road to the restaurant in Rob's classic hunter green Jaguar, they made small talk, mostly about the music industry. She was impressed with his insights, while at the same time aware that he was avoiding any more personal discussion. Maybe he wanted to talk about the two of them at dinner, she thought hopefully.

During dinner the conversation flowed smoothly and with every moment she was more convinced of their compatibility. Surely, she reflected, he, too, must feel that their chemistry, coupled with their mutual interests and natural camaraderie made them an ideal couple.

The restaurant, Geoffrey's, was perched upon a cliff overlooking the Pacific. The waves that surged along the beach below were illuminated by spotlights. A small jazz band played softly in an adjoining room, adding to the subdued yet sophisticated ambiance.

By the time the wine arrived, Callie decided to be bold. "I'd like to propose a toast."

Rob looked at her from across the table, his eyebrows raised in question.

"To honesty."

From the expression on his face, she assumed he had understood her meaning.

"Okay. I'll drink to that."

Their crystal wineglasses clinked in the dimly lit restaurant.

"You know, I have to admit"—Rob's voice was soft and as smooth as the wine—"you're a lot different than I thought you'd be when we first met."

"Well, surely you didn't believe that gossip in the fan magazines."

"Oh, no." He laughed. "One would have to be extremely naive to believe half of what's printed. It's just that you're so exuberant onstage, I didn't expect you to be so sensitive and sincere. I guess your stage presence is so convincing, I believed the image you projected."

"That's all a part of the act," Callie confessed. At first she was amazed at Rob's perception of her vulnerability but realized that it shouldn't surprise her. She felt as if they knew each other.

"I have a confession to make," Rob continued. "Before I saw you this evening, I had every intention of telling you that I thought it would be best if we not see each other anymore."

Callie sat rigid in her seat. She barely noticed the scrumptious smells of the coq au vin the waiter had placed in front of her. Every thread of her being was focused on Rob's handsome face and his intense gaze.

He looked away from her for a moment. She stared at the pale purple orchids in the crystal vase at the center of the table, not daring to look at his face. She knew there was more to come, and yearned for him to alter his conclusion. He must! He had to be feeling how right the two of them were.

He sighed and then continued. "On a rational level everything's going against us. Yet, every time I'm with you I feel alive again. All the pain of the past few years seems to disappear. There's something about the space we share, the way I feel when our eyes meet, the joy I experience when we're together."

Her spirits soared and she felt a heavy load had been lifted from her. She extended her hand to touch his. A sweeping sensation rushed over her, warming every part of her body. By the gleam in his eyes she could tell that he was feeling it too.

"But Callie." He gently pulled away, pushing his shrimp scampi around his plate thoughtfully before continuing. "My head keeps telling me it can't work. You're too much like Gloria—you're married to your career."

"You're wrong about that, Rob. That's not all I care about. Singing is my job; it's not my life. If only I were as good with words as you are. Then maybe I could begin to tell you how much I care about you. I care about us, Rob, about making things work. And I know they can. If you just give them a chance."

"I'd like to believe that, Callie, but I'm not so sure."

Her eyes sought his, pleading her cause from the depths of her heart. She reached for his hand again, once more aware of the electricity that was being generated every time they touched. She questioned in a hushed voice, "Can you deny that you're feeling what I'm feeling at this moment?"

He laughed and gave her hand an affectionate squeeze. "Are you kidding? I couldn't possibly deny it. But I'm afraid of where it's going to lead."

"Give it a chance, Rob. Please, let's give it a chance." She stared at him, willing him to go along with her.

"When I'm with you, I feel as if I don't have any other alternative, Callie. And even when I'm not with you, I can't seem to get you off my mind."

His confession brought on waves of relief. So it wasn't one-sided; so he did share her feelings.

"Is there something wrong with your dinner, miss?"

The appearance of the waiter interfered with her train of thought but not with the exuberance she was feeling at the moment.

"Oh, no, everything is perfect," she replied, star-

ing at the barely touched mushroom-covered con-
coction that filled her plate.

"Just checking." He retreated.

"Maybe you should try a few bites of that," Rob
offered. "I'd hate to have you waste away to nothing."

"Only if you'll help me."

"With pleasure." He beamed at her. The look in
his eyes made her pulse race.

She playfully fed him with her fork and they
lapped down the spicy dish with delight. When
the waiter reappeared to inquire if they wanted
dessert, Callie responded, "Oh, I couldn't, but you
go ahead if you'd like," she added, looking at Rob.

"No, no. I'm going to have to jog an extra mile
as it is to work this off."

As the waiter prepared the check, Rob inquired,
"Are you sure there's nothing you'd like—a liquer,
some coffee, or something?"

"Well, actually, there is something I'd like . . ."

"Yes?"

"Yes! I'd like a walk on the beach."

Rob raised his eyebrows. "Mmm, that's a great
idea! It's a bit chilly, but I've a blanket in the
trunk of my car."

As they made their way down the steep wooden
staircase leading to the beach, Callie was grateful
she had worn boots. She didn't want a rerun of
their last episode on the beach. However, jogging
was the furthest thing from her mind tonight.
This appeared to be the case for Rob as well as he
led her slowly along the shore, one arm swung
over her shoulder.

She couldn't remember the last time she had walked on the beach at night, or the last time she had felt so wonderfully light-headed. Rob's words over dinner were still fresh in her mind, and she needed no further reassurance as to his feelings. The sound of the waves crashing against the shore coupled with the surging sea that extended before them made her feel as if they were the only two people on earth. And the feeling was sublime.

When they arrived at a natural cove, Rob lowered the blanket to the ground, with Callie silently helping. Seconds later they were upon it, clinging together. Their lips found each other's and Callie lost herself in the urgency of Rob's kiss. Soon the sound of the nearby sea was obliterated by the thudding of her heart; the tingle of the damp sea mist was overpowered by the screaming joy igniting all of her senses; and the glorious black velvet night was overshadowed by the rapidly rushing whirlpools she was drowning in as Rob thrust his tongue into her mouth.

Responding with all the pent-up passion of the past weeks, Callie pulled him nearer and raked her fingers down his hard back. She felt his hand cup her breast and her senses thrilled at its touch. She longed to be free of her clothes and feel his skin on her naked body, but the place was not right and the night air was too cool.

She felt his lips moving lightly along her cheek until his tongue smothered her ear in exploration. Waves of ecstasy surged through her body, and she moaned aloud in delight.

"Callie. Callie." His words were whispered between gasping breaths in her ear. "Oh, Callie, I can't tell you how much I've wanted to do this all evening."

He kissed her again, and this time his hand caressed her breast, moving to where he must have felt the rapid beating of her heart. Every inch of her body reeled with pleasure. Every part of her being sang out with the passion she was feeling.

When they pulled away for breath, Callie heard the sound of giggling. Instantaneously, she and Rob turned, only to find two young boys nearby. Aware that they had been seen, the boys slipped away, but she and Rob had been abruptly reminded that they were not alone.

"So much for moonlit splendor." Rob's voice was gentle and loving.

"I didn't even know there was a moon tonight," Callie confessed, gazing into the sky.

"Just a sliver." Rob pointed out the graceful crescent.

"I hadn't noticed before," Callie admitted impishly.

"I hadn't noticed a lot of things before tonight." Rob planted a tender kiss on her nose. "However, I have a session at six tomorrow, and best be getting you home."

"But tomorrow's Saturday!" Callie protested.

"Tell that to Lance Eddenberg."

"Not *the* Lance Eddenberg, the one who's directing *West of Paradise?*"

"The very one. I'm doing the soundtrack for the film."

She was impressed but disappointed that the evening had to come to an end. However, as they strolled back to the car with his arm snugly draped over her shoulder and hers around his waist, he suggested they get together after his session the following day. She wasn't too sad, knowing she would be with him again in a few hours.

So ended the first of several wonderful nights together. As the weeks went by, Rob and Callie spent every moment they could with each other. Seeking privacy, they intentionally patronized out-of-the-way places. They didn't want their relationship splattered all over the press.

Callie believed she was convincing Rob that, as she had insisted, they could make it work. She kept pushing Sizzle's upcoming tour into the back of her mind, almost hoping that if she forgot it, it would go away.

One day, after Callie had not seen Rob for a few evenings, he called at the studio to tell her that he had a surprise for her that evening. As she carefully dressed for the occasion, she wondered what it might be.

That night she decided to wear an especially sexy dress of deep red velvet. Red was her favorite color. She was feeling daring, and its plunging neckline left little to the imagination.

As she carefully applied the bright crimson lipstick, she thought of the way Rob's full lips felt on hers. Her eyes, accented by smoky gray shadow, were sparkling with eagerness. She was sure that tonight would be something special.

She was about to clasp her necklace, when she heard the sound of the buzzer. She dropped the necklace and hurried to the door.

Rob stood before her, more handsome than ever. The smile that beamed in his eye was reflected in the warmth of his welcoming kiss. She clung to him as if they had been separated for weeks rather than days. Thirstily, she drank in his fiery kisses as she ran her fingers through his impossibly thick hair.

Her heart was beating out of control as he lowered his lips to sigh into her ear, "Oh, you smell so glorious, and you look more wonderful than you smell."

He pulled her away from him. She became aware of his dancing eyes scrutinizing her body. She knew she had not needed to apply the blush after all, for surely her face must be flushed.

"I've missed you," she said, smiling.

"And I you. But I feel as if you were with me all the while." He met her gaze with his deep blue eyes.

"I have been."

"I believe you. I was walking by a little shop today and something in the window clearly called out your name to me."

He reached into the pocket of his sport coat and pulled out a package wrapped in gold paper with a red bow.

"A surprise. For you."

"But it's not even Christmas."

"Oh, really? You could have fooled me these past few weeks. I always thought a person could feel this high only at Christmas or on a birthday. And my birthday isn't until May."

Callie took the package, hugging Rob in appreciation. "You're wonderful."

"Now, don't get carried away yet. You haven't seen what's inside."

Feeling as if she were Sweet Sixteen once again, Callie tore open the package. She gasped when she lifted the lid of the velvet jewelry box. Inside, on the end of an intricate gold chain was a beautiful charm. It was a G clef with a sparkling ruby set in it. A series of musical notes each with a ruby chip in them extended on delicate gold bars from the G clef.

"It's gorgeous! It's wonderful! I don't know what to say!"

"I think you just said it."

"Oh, Rob, thank you!" She flung her arms around him, her lips smothering his with appreciation.

"Here, let me put it on you. It goes perfectly with what you're wearing. It's almost as if you planned it."

As Rob fastened the necklace he gently pushed her hair aside. The touch of his fingers on her exposed neck made her squirm in delight.

"I'm so glad you like this. I want you to wear this when you meet my parents at Thanksgiving."

"Your parents?"

"Yes. In fact, the whole family is coming to town and I'm so excited about them meeting you," he replied. Backing away, he observed, "That looks great."

Callie felt her body tighten and was aware of the tension in her jaw.

"Callie, what's wrong?"

She had dreaded this moment, and now that it had arrived, she cursed under her breath. It couldn't have come at a worse time.

"Callie, say something. Surely you're not afraid of my family, are you? They'll love you!"

"Uhm, Rob"—she knew she couldn't put it off any longer; she had put it off too long already— "I think there's something I'd better tell you. I won't be here for Thanksgiving."

"You won't *what?*" He looked at her in amazement, the previous glow in his eyes turning to alarm.

"Rob, I won't be here for Thanksgiving. Sizzle's tour is starting."

"For God's sake, Callie, why didn't you tell me? Why did you wait until now, just days away, to break this to me?"

"Well, I had no idea your family was coming to town."

"But Callie, even if they weren't, don't you think I'd want to spend Thanksgiving with you?"

His face was clouded in fury, his lips tight. He turned away from her.

A stormy silence prevailed until he spun around, and with a voice raspy with contempt uttered, "This is exactly what I was afraid of. It's the same thing over again. It's the same garbage I had to put up with from Gloria."

"But I'm not Gloria and I wish you'd stop comparing us!"

"You're not, huh? You think that being on the road over the holidays is a committed relationship? I don't. I think it stinks. The hell with me! No, your career comes first."

"Rob, this tour has been planned for months. I had no say in the matter."

"It was planned for months, huh?" Now his eyes were glaring in her direction. She felt as if the rage in his gaze could burn her. "Then why did you wait to tell me? If I hadn't mentioned my family's visit, when would you have told me, Callie? When? Can you tell me that?"

"I would have told you sooner, but I was afraid you might act irrationally. I just had no idea how irrational you could be!"

"Irrational? It's irrational to want to be with the woman you care about during holidays? If that's irrational, I'd hate to think what you'd consider rational!"

He clenched his fists and drew his breath, his lips tightening. She was shocked by his reaction.

The color was drained from his face as he muttered icily, "Have a nice Thanksgiving, Callie. And a nice life."

Without another word he was out the door.

Feeling as if she would crumple from misery, she dashed to her bedroom, hot tears streaming down her face. She grabbed the necklace and flung it onto her dressing table. It collided with the other necklace she had originally meant to wear that evening before the buzzer sounded. How long ago that seemed. How long ago and far away.

Chapter Seven
❖ ❖ ❖

PORTLAND WAS COLD and drizzly. Seattle failed to charm her, as it only reminded Callie of Rob's home. Vancouver remained but a dismal memory. The gloomy skies of the Pacific Northwest matched her mood, and the foghorns kept her awake nights after the concerts.

Sizzle had performed at the British Columbia Pavilion on Thanksgiving, and although the audience had given them an enthusiastic reception, it didn't lift her spirits. Callie was unable to forget that while all across the United States families were gathered around the table delighting in the festive holiday, it was just another Thursday night for Canadians. She couldn't help but think about Rob and the damage she had caused.

Callie had not seen or spoken with him since

their argument the night he had given her the necklace, nor had she been able to get him out of her mind. If only she could forget him! But as she stood before a myriad of blurred faces at San Francisco's Fillmore West a week later, wailing the words of "Class Reunion," she could see no face other than his.

"Memories time can't erase . . .".

Although they had spent mere weeks together, the memories were still fresh in her mind and the song intensified them. She had to hold back her tears. The audience couldn't possibly know that the emotion she put into the words was genuine.

Callie was relieved when they finished the song Rob had written and switched to the more upbeat "Razor's Edge." As the title suggested, her nerves were becoming frazzled.

Past tours had been exciting, but now she was merely going through the motions. Everything felt unreal—so rushed and frenzied. No doubt about it, the glamour was gone and all that remained was the reality of exhausting performances, airport terminals, and stiff white sheets in impersonal hotel rooms to greet her when the day was over.

How she wished Rob were there for her as he had been just weeks before. How she longed to snuggle up to him late at night and feel his lips upon hers. She wondered if his sister was among the howling audience. She recalled seeing her picture in his house. She was blond like himself, but lighter and with paler eyes. Oh, how she longed to see his deep blue eyes again. She scolded herself at the thought.

She could hear her wispy soprano voice blend in with the lead guitar and electric piano as she sang out the final lines of the song. More than ever she was aware of the effort it was taking to carry off the tune. Knowing the set would soon be over, she sang the last bars of "Razor's Edge" with renewed energy. The audience broke into a flood of applause, screams, and whistles. Callie blew kisses to the crowd, and although she smiled radiantly, she felt drained. She rushed off the stage with the band surrounded by well-wishers, autograph seekers, and members of the media.

"We've got to do an encore!" Lynne joyfully gushed as they made their way to the wings.

That meant performing "Can Spend the Day Just Looking in Your Eyes," a song Lynne and Guy had written for each other. Although Callie considered it the weakest number on Sizzle's upcoming album, to appease the couple she had agreed to include it on the tour. Tension had been escalating within the group now that it appeared doubtful that Electric would be renewing their contract.

"Don't look so thrilled about the encore," Ken whispered in her ear, his sarcasm not being lost on what she knew must have been her sour expression.

"It's just that I'm really tired," she confessed to him as they made their way back onstage.

"Don't worry, kiddo. I'm sure you'll manage to get through it."

Although Ken winked at her encouragingly, his comments didn't help. Every note on this tour was becoming a laborious effort.

When the final number was over, the audience reluctantly allowed them to depart. Callie could feel her body shaking, the exhaustion of the day catching up with her. The entire tour had been one draining performance after another with no time to catch her breath in between.

She sank into her seat on the limousine, closed her eyes, and tried to block out the excited babbling of the other members of the group, only too aware that at one time she, too, had felt exhilarated after successful concerts. No more.

"And I'm sure they would have had us there all night if they could have," Lynne said, grinning with pride.

"That should give Electric something to think about," Tom boasted.

"Well, I hate to put a damper on your enthusiasm," Vic cut in, "but while the crowds were responsive, the turnout has been disappointing. Unfortunately, the whole tour has been like this. And I don't have to remind you, but that's what the big shots at Electric will be looking at. That and the reviews, which haven't been anything to write home about."

It was Vic. Good old practical Vic, Callie thought to herself. And yet she knew it was all too true. Turnouts had not been as high as they had hoped, and reviews had been bleak despite the audience's reaction. The crowds had responded with conviction in Seattle, and yet the reviews had been tepid. She hoped the reporters from the *San Francisco Chronicle* and the *Oakland Tribune* would treat them more kindly.

"Yeah, but *Rocking Stone* loved Callie, and they're the big word around this town," Greg Green said with satisfaction, fiddling with the gold pinky ring on his little finger. Greg had been the assistant manager and jack-of-all-trades ever since Callie could remember. While his slick manner was not endearing to her, he knew the business and had gotten them a lot of good publicity.

"Yes, they loved Callie," Vic confirmed. "How could anyone not love Callie?" He patted her hand affectionately. "Unfortunately, Electric didn't love two songs on *Sizzle Sizzles Over*. Not only are we going to have to substitute them, but they want remakes on three others."

"Oh, no! That means weeks back in the studio." Lynne frowned. "Which songs did they reject?" Vic told them with resignation in his voice.

Relieved that they weren't Rob's, Callie let out a deep sigh.

"Wow, Callie, you look more zonked than I've ever seen you." Lynne's assessment hardly lifted her downhearted spirits. "Maybe a few drinks will cheer you up. We're having a little get-together in our suite. We all need something after this news. Why don't you join us?"

"Oh, I just don't think I'm up to it tonight." Callie sighed. Privately, she thought that the last

thing she needed was to be around the rest of the
band. What had once given her so much satisfaction was now becoming a trial.

"Well, I'm sure a hot bath and good night's sleep
will make everything look better," Vic offered.

But as they strolled into the lobby of the Hyatt
Regency, Callie doubted it. With much effort she
forced a tight smile for the photographers, who
pounced on her in the ultramodern lobby. Vic
detoured them from the restless journalists, but
she couldn't keep her shoulders from slouching
as she broke away from the group and dragged
her feet toward the glass-enclosed elevators. Normally, she adored the hotel's lobby, with its slick,
sweeping elegance, but tonight all she could think
of was collapsing in the privacy of her room.

"I know what you need," Tom's annoyingly familiar voice came from behind.

Wearily, she turned in his direction and sighed.
"Like the man suggested, a hot bath and good
night's rest."

"I don't think it's rest you need, baby."

"Oh, Tom, I'm too tired to play word games
with you."

"It wasn't games I had in mind."

To illustrate his point, he pulled her into a
crushing embrace. She felt his rough face upon
hers, and although she struggled to get free, his
grip was more than she could handle.

"Let go, Tom. Are you nuts? Let go!"

"Hey, what's the matter? Our shining star isn't
quite herself tonight."

Wrestling to get free of him, she became aware of the flash of camera bulbs nearby. Damn those photographers—couldn't they ever leave her alone?

"Look, Tom. It's been a long day. We're all tired. Get some sleep. Anyway, where's Elana?" She was Tom's live-in girlfriend.

"She split. So now you and I can have a little fun."

Callie was grateful for the sudden appearance of Ken, who had been in the other limousine. During the years she had been with Sizzle, Tom had made advances toward her before, usually when he was between girlfriends, but she had always been able to simply laugh them off. Tonight, however, she was not in the mood for his shenanigans.

"Hey, you two. How about joining us in Lynne and Guy's room for a little party?"

"Thanks anyway, Ken, but I'm exhausted."

"Yeah, our Callie here is in a real sour mood."

"Lay off, Tom. We're all a bit uptight when we're on the road."

"Yeah, well, I'm all for partying. I bet there'll be some foxy chicks there." Tom glared in Callie's direction.

All she could manage was a feeble "Have fun," relieved to be free of him. Thank goodness for Ken. In all the years she had been with Sizzle, she was aware of Ken's protectiveness toward her. Whether it was because he had brought her into the group or because of an unspoken crush he might have on her, she didn't know. But she had always valued his friendship.

She went up to her bedroom, which, unlike the elegant lobby, was nondescript. She sighed—how empty it was—how alone she was feeling. She quickly undressed and ran a bath. She soaked in the steamy tub and tried to clear her mind. But it didn't help.

Nothing seemed to help, she admitted to herself later as she tossed and turned in the sheets trying to sleep. She couldn't get her mind off Rob. His blue eyes appeared in front of her and her pulse began racing. She recalled the way his lips felt upon hers.

Suddenly, she heard a loud knock on her door. Its pounding reverberated throughout the muted darkness, causing her to stiffen in fear. Who could it be? Why would anyone be pounding on her door at this hour?

Not knowing whether to call out in the stillness of the night or simply ignore the intrusion, she remained frozen in her bed, her heart pounding in trepidation. What should she do? Before she could make any decision, the knocking began once again, this time louder than before.

"Who's there?" she called.

"Open the door!" the familiar male voice demanded.

Oh, no! It was Tom! Why couldn't he leave her alone?

She pounced out of bed, threw on her robe, and attached the chain lock. Opening the door the few inches the chain would allow, she called out in a hushed but angry voice, "Tom—go away. I'm tired. I want to get some sleep."

"Oh, come on, Callie baby. Let me in. Just for a minute."

"Tom, why don't you get some strong black coffee and try to sober up. We still have one last appearance and you'd better be sober for it."

"Why ya getting so uptight, baby? I just wanted to see if you wanna join the party."

"The answer is no and good night!"

Callie slammed the door, irate that Tom had annoyed her. It would be harder than ever to sleep now that she was so wound up.

She wished there were someone she could talk to at that moment. With the exception of Ken, she realized how distant she felt from the other members of Sizzle. And because Ken had a crush on her, it wasn't fair to burden him with this.

And Vic, while he was a good friend, had his own problems trying to find a record company to take them in.

Although her body ached with fatigue, her mind was more alert than ever as she lay between the stiff cold sheets. She had lost the man she really cared about because of her commitment to a bunch of people who had once existed quite well without her. This revelation kept her awake for most of the night.

Things seemed no brighter the next morning and the bags under her eyes were testimony to another sleepless night. Her attempt to cover them with makeup only emphasized her washed-out appearance.

As she entered the hotel lobby, she hoped to keep a low profile but immediately was accosted by camera bulbs popping, and her weary eyes darted in their direction. The photographer looked familiar. It was then, as she took a closer glance at the bald, wiry photographer that she knew where she had seen him before—in Los Angeles, at the interview with *Rocking Stone.*

"I thought you already had all the pictures you needed," she challenged him.

"That was then, sweetheart. This is now. Besides, I'm not working for *Rocking Stone* anymore." He continued to snap shots as he talked. "I'm with *Pop Star.* "

Callie wondered at his change since she considered this as a step down but couldn't possibly voice this opinion. Before she could say anything else, she felt a pair of arms pulling her into an unwanted embrace from behind, followed by a sloppy kiss planted on her neck.

"Oh, baby! Did you ever miss a party last night!"

"Tom! Knock it off!"

She squirmed away from him, but not before the ambitious photographer had snapped more shots.

Exasperated, she felt like screaming "Why can't you all leave me alone?" But she already had the answer to that question: it was the price she paid for being a star.

Oh, how she hated being on the road! She despised the lack of privacy. She was grateful that this was the last night of the tour.

Suddenly, she realized she never wanted to go on the road again! Surprised at her own reaction, she wondered whether this was how she truly felt.

Chapter Eight
❖ ❖ ❖

THINGS CHANGE, you know that, Callie. Just because you loved being on the road at one time doesn't mean you're always going to feel that way."

Callie sipped her white wine as she watched Sharon, in awe of her culinary skills. Her friend was perched next to the stove, stirring spaghetti sauce in one pot as homemade applesauce for the baby simmered on another burner. As soon as the tour ended, Callie had sought refuge and advice in her best friend's home.

"But I can tell that's not all that's bothering you, is it?"

"No," Callie confessed. "There's trouble with Electric, but I don't want to bore you with that."

"I don't find it at all boring. After spending the day feeding the ducks at the park, it sounds rather exciting to me."

"It does, huh? Somehow I think I'd rather have

spent the day with Eric feeding the ducks at the park." Callie was surprised to discover how true these words rang—truer than she ever could have imagined. "You wouldn't believe the pressure at these remake sessions now that it looks as if Electric won't be renewing our contract. The tension was so thick today you could cut it with that butcher's knife you're holding."

"It's that bad, huh?" Sharon chopped mushrooms and flung them into the spaghetti sauce, which was sending its spicy aroma through the kitchen.

"Oh, Sharon, you have no idea. The possibility that we may not get another contract has gotten everyone in the group unnerved, but their egos are too inflated to admit it."

"But you'll be able to sign with someone else, won't you?"

"Who knows? Vic's working on it. But a lot will depend on our new album, especially the video. Sometimes it takes a while to get another contract. And that means time without a recording studio and an album, which could be a disaster."

"But Sizzle does so well on the road!"

"That's just what I'm afraid of! They think we could draw bigger crowds in the Midwest, but that would mean a major tour—at least six weeks on the road. Everyone wants it except me. Really, Sharon, I don't think I could stand it!"

A pensive expression came over Sharon's face. "Listen, I might have the perfect solution for you. Doug was looking through *Variety* for some film editing work and he came across an item that he thought might interest you."

She placed her wooden spoon on the slick ceramic counter and handed Callie the current copy of *Variety*.

Callie scanned the words: "Singer/actress wanted for prime-time television show. Must have experience. Prefer blonde, twenties. 555-9867. Ask for Ellen Falk."

"But what about Sizzle?" Callie demanded.

"What about them?" Sharon shrugged her shoulders. "You just said the contract hasn't been renewed and might not be. The rest of the group delights in touring, and you don't. Besides, as much as I love you, Callie, you know you're replaceable."

What Sharon was saying rang true, yet Callie still had her doubts. "But I haven't done any acting recently."

"Oh, come on now. You had parts in two shows. Besides, if you notice, they seem to be stressing 'singer.'"

Callie reread the ad. "Maybe I should call them," she mused. "But I'd need to do it through an agent who handles actresses. Mine only represents singers."

"No sweat." Sharon grabbed a piece of paper and jotted down a number. "Here, call her, she'll help." Sharon observed Callie for a moment before continuing. "Okay, now that we've solved your career problems, let's move on to something more interesting. Like the other thing that's bothering you?"

Callie sighed and gave out a small laugh of acknowledgment. "You know me too well."

"I should, after all these years. Let me see—I'd be willing to bet the first name begins with an 'R' and the last with an 'M.' "

"Is it that obvious?"

"Oh, Callie, face it—you haven't been the same since the night he walked out your door!"

Giving a deep sigh, Callie admitted, "Yeah, you're right. And it's worse now than ever. On the tour I knew there was no chance of running into him, but since I've been back I can't help looking for him everyplace I go."

As the evening wore on and she watched the loving interchange among Sharon's family, she became more aware of her own loneliness. She couldn't help feeling like an alien from another planet—her life was so different from the harmonious scene she witnessed that evening. Was this what she wanted? Would a life like Sharon and Doug's make her happy?

When Callie entered the studio the following day, the group was clustered around Vic. Everyone was talking at once.

"Hi, guys, what's up?"

"Another tour . . ."

"Oh, no, not another tour!" Callie expressed her dismay. "We just got back from a tour!"

"So there's no law against going on the road again." Tom gave her a wry smile. "What's the matter—you hot for some guy here in town?"

Callie felt her cheeks growing warm but ignored the comment. "I don't see why we have to think about going on the road again so soon."

"But the last tour was for only five weeks," Lynne intervened. "We're talking about a big one now—one that will really give us the publicity we need."

"Yeah," Guy agreed, "give Electric something to think about."

"But they still might renew our contract," Callie said.

"But it's rather peculiar that they haven't done it already," Vic said.

"And think how good it would look if they knew we had a major tour in the making," Guy appealed to her.

"I don't think they'd care that much about that," Callie said in opposition. "I would think they'd be more concerned about the outcome of *Sizzle Sizzles Over* and the response to the video."

"Well, it still wouldn't hurt us to start thinking about another tour," Ken stated.

Speak for yourself, Callie thought. Before she could say anything, Vic came to her rescue. "I think Callie has a good point. We've got to concentrate on getting this material down, so let's get on with the session and leave the tour talk for later."

Grateful that that discussion was temporarily postponed, Callie concentrated on her singing. At the first break she scurried to a telephone and dialed the number of the agent Sharon had given her to arrange for an audition for the television role. She felt guilty, but it was obvious that everyone in the group thrived on constant traveling except for her. Besides, Sharon was right—she was replaceable.

When she explained to the agent what she wanted, there was a noticeable silence on the other end of the line.

"Is there anything wrong?" Callie inquired.

"Oh, no. No. It's just that I'm a bit surprised. I didn't know you were looking for a job."

"I just discovered it myself," Callie confessed with a sudden surge of conviction overtaking her. Of course! Why hadn't she seen it before? She was ready for a change, and this just could be what she needed.

The next few days were draining. Not only had she become more aware of the distance that had formed between her and the other members of the group, but her longing for Rob increased steadily. By Saturday she was thankful to have the day off from recording. But all she could think of was Rob.

Sunday was worse. Memories of the Sundays they had spent together flooded her: leisurely mornings in reading the papers, afternoon rides along the coast, quiet romantic dinners. She pictured him as he appeared the last time he had come to her door, so handsome and relaxed in his casual clothes. She could still recall the way he had held her in his arms and the thrilling sensations when he kissed her.

She took out an album by Barbara Stenton, which had Rob's hit song "I Remember" on it. She placed it on the stereo and played it over and over. Yes, she, too, remembered—oh, how she re-membered.

This was too much. She couldn't stand the si-lence between them any longer. Impulsively, she grabbed the telephone and began dialing his num-ber. Just as she was about to punch the last but-ton, she froze. The image of Rob scowling at her returned. Dammit! Why had he been so unreason-able? If he cared, which obviously he didn't, he would reach out and call her. How could he have thrown it all out so easily? No! She couldn't go through with it! She slammed down the receiver and burst into tears that lasted throughout the day and well into the night.

When Monday dawned, Callie appreciated the bustling activity of the studio after the tormenting solitude of her empty house. She was grateful for the hectic day that stretched ahead. She hoped the demanding recording session and the audition for the television show would help get her mind off Rob.

The recording session went smoothly, but by the time she found herself in the private audition room studying her lines in the script for "Trinity Bluff," her nerves were taut. She knew she was on shaky ground but dared not let her anxiety show.

When she entered the slickly decorated office, Callie was greeted by Ellen Falk, the casting direc-tor. Ellen was a stocky woman, intently serious in appearance, her most prominent feature being oversize glasses that masked her nervously dart-ing eyes.

Ellen introduced Callie to the three men who were seated in the room, all of whom were casually and expensively attired. Ted, the producer, extended a firm handshake to her. He was bearded and had dark eyes that met hers as he took her hand. Roy, the assistant producer, was slender and fair. He jumped to his feet to shake her hand. The director, Claude, merely gave her a tight, close-lipped smile from across the room.

Ellen cleared her throat and proceeded in a businesslike tone. "Well, I hope you've had enough time to go over the script. I realize you haven't seen it before, but we allotted you the same amount of time as the other actors."

Callie felt her anxiety rising. Her palms were beginning to sweat. She hoped her mascara hadn't run and that her nose wasn't shining like the bald spot on Claude's head. True, she had read for parts in the past, but that seemed like years ago. More than ever, she was aware of how badly she wanted this role, how ready she was for a change in her life.

Determined to mask her insecurity, she took a deep breath and directed her attention to the script. Within seconds it was as if Callie had vanished and Brigette, the disillusioned young nightclub singer in love with Drew, a magnetic and dangerous gambler who was a notorious womanizer, had taken her place.

"And I suppose you were alone the night your phone was off the hook? You expect me to believe that, do you? What do you take me for—some kind of fool?"

She so empathized with Brigette that anger overtook her and her body began to tremble. She pretended that she was speaking to her handsome costar rather than to the skinny, effeminate assistant producer who was reading Drew's part.

"Liar! Liar! Liar!" She screamed the final words with such intensity that the script nearly dropped from her hands.

Silence hung in the room for what seemed like an eternity. She allowed the script to fall slowly to her side. She was exhausted from the energy she had put into the reading. Afraid to look up or break the hush, she said nothing, but she could hear her heart pounding anxiously.

"That was quite good." Ellen's voice sounded frail yet noncommittal.

Ted joined in, "Yes, quite good. We know you can sing rock, but on 'Trinity Bluff' Brigette would hardly be singing rock, so we would like to hear you sing a standard."

"No problem," Callie assured him. "I was raised on standards. Anything in particular you'd like me to do?"

"How about 'That Old Feeling'? We have a copy of it here."

As Ted produced the music, Ellen rambled on. "I know this is a bit unorthodox—not giving you time to prep and all—but we're asking all the actors auditioning for the role to sightread."

Callie noted an apologetic sound in her voice and assured her that it was no problem. Although she rarely sang a cappella, nothing came easier, especially since she knew the song. This time there were no butterflies and no uncertain feelings when she completed the song. She knew she had been good.

"Nicely done," Ted informed her.

"I'll say," Roy added, to which Callie noticed the director throwing him a sour look.

"Well, yes." Ellen's attempt at objectivity was in vain. "Very good. But I'll be honest with you, I'm feeling a bit leery about some things. Are you sure that this is what you want? Are you sure you want to give up the excitement of performing before live audiences and being on the road?"

The last words made her answer come easily. "Oh, I'm sure. I'm ready for a change. In fact, I'm overready."

"Have you discussed this with your group yet?" Ted inquired.

"Not yet," Callie confessed. "I don't feel I need to say anything until I know whether or not I get the part."

"Well, we certainly won't be able to tell you anything about that for several days. We have quite a few actors to audition."

Callie detected the cool professionalism in Ellen's voice and she couldn't help but wonder if the casting director doubted the sincerity of her response to her questions. Or perhaps she hadn't been impressed by the reading.

"Of course," Callie replied. Her heart sank as her confidence diminished. While she knew that her singing had been sensational, she had no idea whether the audition as a whole had gone well.

"What concerns me is whether your leaving the

band will present any problems." It was Ted's dubious voice again.

Callie took a deep breath before continuing. She wanted to answer properly. "Uhm, what I understood from my previous conversation with Ms. Falk was that the job doesn't start for a few months. That would give Sizzle plenty of time to find a replacement."

"Well, yes, I suppose it would." Ellen cleared her throat and gazed around the room before continuing. "If you have no questions, I believe we've covered everything, wouldn't you say so, gentlemen?"

They all nodded their heads in agreement. Callie felt the dryness in her throat. She had several questions, but none that she could ask. Had they liked her? Had the audition gone well? She had absolutely no idea. She merely thanked them for their time and left the room feeling rather bewildered.

The studio was buzzing when Callie returned from the audition. Immediately, she sensed that something was in the air.

"Wait'll you catch a look at this," Guy called out from across the room.

Lynne waved a piece of paper in her direction. Callie glanced at it, the bold graphic letterhead with the word *Playmate* jumping off the page at her.

"*Playmate?* What ever could they want with us?"

"Hardly with us, sweetheart." Tom's ironic gaze

swept over her. "With you. They want to feature you in the March issue—centerfold and all!"

Callie felt her mouth drop. "You must be kidding!"

"Just think of what great publicity it would be!" Lynne gushed.

"You mean to tell me you would do that?" Callie was astonished at Lynne's response.

"Hell, yes!"

Guy chimed in, "Hey, I think it's great—a real compliment."

"Well, I don't!" Callie glanced over at Vic for support. "I'm not even going to consider it."

"Let's just cool it, all of you. It's Callie's decision anyway."

"She could at least consider it," Guy implored. "After all, it would be good for the group."

"I don't know"—Tom glared at her— "Callie doesn't seem to care all that much for the group these days."

She felt like challenging his remark by stating that it appeared that the group didn't care too much for her feelings these days either, but before she could, he added, "Whoever thought she'd turn into such a prude!"

She knew his remark had been triggered by her rejection of him in San Francisco, so she said nothing and merely gave him a dirty look.

"Hey, what's going on?" Ken said, entering the studio.

When Vic explained the dilemma, Ken responded, "I don't blame her for not wanting to pose for them. Some things are still sacred."

"Like getting on with the session, I believe," Vic was quick to point out. "Come on, everybody. Let's get back to work. We're on a very tight schedule here, you know."

"Well, I know that," Tom returned, "but I wonder if Callie's aware of it. That was quite a long lunch break she took."

"Knock it off, Tom. She told us she had an appointment, and besides, we've been getting drum tracks down while she was gone. We haven't lost any time."

Relieved that the discussion had ended, and appreciative that at least Vic and Ken supported her decision not to pose for *Playmate*, she was glad to resume her place at the microphone.

"Oh, by the way, Callie"—Vic approached her and whispered in her ear—"I'd like you to stop by my office when the session's over. There's something I'd like you to see."

Callie wondered what it could be that Vic wanted to show her. Her high regard for him was causing her to feel a pang of guilt about the audition. Maybe she could take him with her, she mused. Stop it, she scolded herself. She was jumping several steps ahead of herself—she hadn't even been offered the part.

As the morning's recordings began, not only Tom but Guy and Lynne were treating her coolly. Although she managed not to let their rejection affect her performance, she was so eager to avoid any discussion of another tour that she rushed from the studio as soon as the day's work ended.

It was only as she climbed into her car that she

recalled the conversation she had had with Vic
and went racing back to the room he used as an
office.

"Oh, I'm so glad you haven't left," she exclaimed.

"I was about to," Vic confessed. "The way you
raced out of the studio, I expected you to be half-
way home by now. I know something's been bothering you and I think I have just the thing to cheer
you up—hot off the press—Rob Matthews's latest
ballad!"

Callie could feel her knees becoming weak. She
had managed to get Rob off her mind for a few
hours. As Vic handed the music sheet to her, she
felt her conviction rapidly waning—the last thing
she was prepared to deal with was Rob's latest
ballad! Still, she couldn't wait to hear it.

She sank into a chair. As she read the lyrics Rob
had written, her heart began to reel and her head
swam in a mass of rekindled emotions.

> *Falling in love every time that you're singing*
> *Falling in love with the telephone ringing*
> *Falling in love all the way*
> *Falling in love all the way . . .*

He had to love her—of course he did! There
could be no doubt about it—the song had to be
written for her! She was as certain of that as she
was of the aching in her heart and the desolate
loneliness she had felt since they'd been apart.

"Thanks, Vic, for showing me this." Callie managed a calm voice, which was difficult considering

the joy that was bubbling in her. She could recall
as if it were but hours ago the way the telephone
had interrupted their first kiss. Of course he had
written the song for her. His ex-wife couldn't
carry a tune; he had told her so on several occasions.

"I thought it might interest you." Vic's voice
sounded compassionate. Callie sensed that he
might know her well-kept secret. But it was all
right if he did—she trusted him.

"You can keep it," he continued, "I think he
wanted you to have it."

Callie thanked him quickly and rushed home.
Every nerve in her body felt alive for the first
time since she and Rob had parted. When she reread the lyrics and hummed along with the notes
in the privacy of her living room, it dawned on
her that she had heard that tune before. Suddenly
she knew where—at Rob's house, the night she
had returned his sweater to him. At that moment
she knew what she had to do.

She reached for the telephone to call Rob, to
tell him that she saw the song, and that she
couldn't get him out of her heart either. She
punched the digits without hesitation. Every
nerve in her body delighted in the rightness of
their love.

She heard him answer and suddenly couldn't
utter a single syllable. She was speechless, over-
whelmed by the sound of his voice.

No, she decided what she had to say was too
important for the telephone. She put down the
receiver and grabbed her car keys. With a surge

of confidence running through her veins, and
feeling more alive than she had felt since their
awful fight, Callie raced along the Pacific Coast
Highway on her way to Rob's Paradise Cove retreat.

Chapter Nine
❖ ❖ ❖

DOUBTS BEGAN TO besiege her as she drove the
winding highway to Rob's house. What if he was
already involved with another woman? What if
he didn't feel the way she did? How could he, she
reflected bitterly—he would have called her if he
did.

She had almost decided to abandon her impulsive visit, when she glanced down at the music
sheet. That song! Didn't it prove that he loved her?

Still, as she swerved along the curving road, she
felt apprehensive. Only the image of Rob clearly
imprinted in her mind and the copy of "Falling in
Love" resting on the car seat next to her reassured
her. When she finally arrived at his house, she
was almost dizzy with anticipation.

She grabbed the lead sheet and dashed to his
door, knowing that if she hesitated, she might
lose her courage.

The instant he appeared, a shadowy presence

behind the screen door, she froze. All the well-planned words she had rehearsed vanished. She remained speechless while an awkward silence enveloped them.

It was Rob's smooth voice that broke the silence. "Callie—is it really you?"

The joy in his voice encouraged her. "I had to see you. Vic gave me a copy of 'Falling in Love' and I couldn't stay away any longer!"

As he opened the door, she thrilled to the sight of him once again. Oh, how she had missed him! He appeared somehow taller and more handsome than before. His thick blond hair was mussed, giving him a casual and sexy look. She longed to run her fingers through it, to throw herself in his arms.

She held his eyes with a deliberate stare. "Rob, I know you weren't lying when you wrote these words."

"No, I wasn't," he admitted. "And I won't lie now and say I can forget you, because I can't. Lord knows I've tried, but I can't." His voice sounded as soft as the night's breeze that was sighing through the entrance. His eyes, deep blue and tender, never let go of hers.

"Oh, Rob, you have no idea of how miserable I've been!" Callie could feel her ragged breath. "The tour was awful. All I could think about was you." She flung herself into his open arms, sobbing, "I've missed you so much!"

She cuddled close to him, basking in the strong comfort of his embrace. He whispered hoarsely,

"Oh, Callie. My Callie. I've missed you too! I know I overreacted that night."

"No, you were right. I should have told you about the tour sooner, especially since I knew how you felt about it. I guess I tried to convince myself that if I pushed it to the back of my mind, it would go away. I just didn't want anything to come between us, but I know now that I should have been honest with you from the start."

The words brought on a flood of relief as she clung even closer in his arms.

"And I shouldn't have been so stubborn." He massaged her back as he said the comforting words. "If you only knew how many times I picked up the phone to call you, but, of course, you were on the road, and I had no idea how to reach you and didn't know when you'd be back—"

His voice broke off as he drew her closer to him. His confession eased her mind. He held her tightly and gazed into her eyes. She could feel her heart beating uncontrollably as her lips naturally parted.

His mouth hungrily enveloped hers. Her senses exploded as the passion she had been denying for so long surfaced. She could feel his chest rapidly heaving with excitement as she tasted the sweetness of his kiss, a sweetness that she had been unable to forget.

As they came together, Callie found herself melting into the strength of Rob's body. She ran her hands up and down his strong arms. She clung to him, never wanting to take the chance of losing him again.

"Oh, Callie. Callie. I've yearned for this moment for so long. . . ." His voice came from the depths of his throat. She could barely hear the words over his heavy breathing.

He scooped her into his arms and carried her to his bedroom. As he lowered her onto his bed, his lips dove to smother hers. He thrust his tongue into her mouth, and as she met it with hers, ripples of pleasure spread throughout her body. She reached under his shirt and felt the radiating warmth of his skin as she massaged his back with her palms.

His hands found her heaving breasts. She felt his tender caresses and arched her back, pressing her burning nipples into his hands. She sensed his fingers unbuttoning her sweater and inhaled the fragrance of her own heady perfume as her body responded to his magnetic touch in the soft night air.

"Callie my love." The sound of his voice, huskier than ever, added to her excitement. "I've missed you so. I've dreamed of this . . . so long . . . so much."

"Oh, Rob." Her words came out as whispers from some part of her she barely knew existed. They were already beyond words—there was no longer a need for them.

Her body reeled with the rising pleasure of his touch. As she rumpled his thick hair with her fingers, her feelings were mounting, becoming more

intense than ever before. She wanted nothing to
separate them again. Nothing.

Submerged in the magnitude of her emotions,
she felt all doubts, all defenses, slipping away. His
touch was assuring—his nearness proof of his
love, and she yearned to make up for lost time.
She explored his earlobe with her tongue. She
tasted a slightly salty flavor as she heard his deep
guttural groans.

Her fingers were tingling from the feel of his
skin as she caressed his back in encouragement.

"Love you . . ." barely escaped from her
throat, to which she heard him moan, "Love you,
too . . . oh, how I love . . ." echoing into her
consciousness. His hands were exploring her wet-
ness, sending irresistible sensations to the innermost parts of her body.

How marvelous he could make her feel! Oh,
how she desired to ride the peaks of their passion
once again—to hold nothing back. Nothing.

Being in Rob's arms again, his warm body upon
her, his breath as uneven as hers, was impelling
her rushing senses beyond control. Nothing else
mattered. All she could feel was the enormous
force of emotion that was sweeping her away like
a leaf in the roaring sea surging just beyond their
window.

Afterward, she fell into a light slumber. When
she awoke, she had no idea how long she had
been asleep. She was alone. She panicked—where
was Rob?

It was then she noticed that the sliding glass
door leading to the deck outside his bedroom was

opened slightly, letting a cool breeze enter the silent room. She could hear the sound of the sea as
distinctly as the feel of Rob's lips still lingering
upon hers. She lifted her body onto her elbows
and caught sight of Rob's muscular frame silhouetted against the crashing sea.

She threw his robe around her naked body and
stepped onto the wooden deck overlooking the
ocean. How wonderful it was that night. Glorious.

"It's beautiful, isn't it?"

His baritone voice assured her that he shared
her feelings as she gazed at his face made visible
by the half moon that had risen above them. He
drew her into his arms.

"Yes, it's beautiful," she agreed.

"As are you," Rob whispered softly in her ear.

They watched the surging sea in silence, Callie
feeling more contented than she ever had before.
Rob broke the silence. "While you were sleeping,
I threw some dinner together. I assume you
haven't eaten yet."

"Oh, you!" Callie teased him. "Always worrying
about me eating. You'd think I was a child."

"Definitely not a child. Children can be made to
eat." He returned her teasing tone.

"Well, okay. If it will make you happy. I'll eat
something. As long as it's not tofu and sprouts. I
remember that time you tried to get me to eat that
stuff."

"You never did know what was good for you!"
He led her to the table on the deck.

"And I suppose you do?" Callie observed the
platter of fresh fruit and cheese that Rob had

placed on the table. The trusty bowl of fruit, she laughed to herself. Fortunately for her, there was pizza, which she immediately seized, ignoring the tossed salad.

"Still haven't changed, have you?" Rob remarked as she ate her pizza.

"Actually, I have. I've changed a lot."

"Oh?" Rob's voice was encouraging and loaded with expectation.

"Yes. This last tour did it. I really hated it, honest I did, Rob. I couldn't begin to tell you how awful it was!"

"Good. Because it was dreadful for me too. Lord only knows I was a beast to be around during Thanksgiving. And Christmas and New Year's were a total blur." He gave out a sigh and continued. "So what are you going to do about it? Or should I say, what are we going to do about it?"

"I'm working on it. Believe me—I'm working on it."

"I want to believe you, Callie," Rob responded meaningfully.

How she longed to tell him about "Trinity Bluff." She knew that if she got the part, she would no longer need to travel. But that was now beyond her control. She had done her best at the audition—all she could do was wait. She wanted that role as much as she wanted to be held in Rob's arms forever. But what if she didn't get the part? Then they would both be disappointed.

"'To us, and to honesty." He lifted his wineglass in her direction, and as their glasses met in mid-air Callie decided that she couldn't keep the audi-

tion a secret. She couldn't let their tenuous recon-
ciliation hinge on any more half truths or
omissions.

"I've always been afraid of honesty," she admitted. "But I realize that it's different with you and
that it's dishonesty that has led to our conflicts in
the past." Callie drew in her breath. "I auditioned
for a major role in 'Trinity Bluff.' "

Rob listened in silence as she told him about
the audition. He smiled at her as a few moments
elapsed before he responded. "That sounds great,
Callie, and I hope you get the part if that's what
you really want. But are you sure about this? And
what about Sizzle?"

"I'm torn there, I have to admit. But if we don't
get a new recording contract, it will mean heavy
touring, and whether I get the part or not, I know
I don't want that again."

"Is that because of us?"

"Only partially. With or without you, I just can't
live like that anymore."

Rob took her hand in his and caressed it.

"Oh, Rob. I don't want us to be apart ever again.
I couldn't stand it—I just couldn't!"

"I couldn't either!" He rose from his chair and
extended his arms in her direction.

She sprang into his embrace, feeling him pull
her close. His reassuring kiss reinforced her already ironclad desire to make things work out.
The ocean crashing just beyond the window was
the only sound in the otherwise still night, and its
presence soon faded as her senses became im-

mersed in the sensations Rob was once again expertly creating in her body.

They maneuvered their way back into the bedroom and made love again. Afterward, Callie fell asleep. She slept more soundly than she had in weeks.

When she arose in the morning, she momentarily forgot where she was. Then, cradled in the shelter of Rob's arms, she felt his firm, warm body next to hers. She flushed with delight as memories of the previous evening's lovemaking returned. She felt his fingers slowly moving up her back, followed by feathery kisses on her forehead and cheek.

But as she further awoke, she became aware that something wasn't right. Her eyes felt itchy and her nose was stuffed. Oh, no, it was her allergies!

"Sagan! How the hell did you get in here?" Rob exclaimed. He had always put the cat out at night.

Callie sniffled. "I guess it doesn't really matter how he got here—he did!"

"Out! Out!" Rob shooed him away.

But of course it was too late. The damage, as confirmed by her weepy eyes and her wheezing nose, had already been done.

"Oh, I'm really sorry, Callie. He must have sneaked in with us last night. I just wasn't paying enough attention. I'm sorry. Really, I am."

"It's not your fault." She recalled that they had been so wrapped up in each other the previous night that Sagan easily could have slipped in unnoticed.

Callie silently pondered her dilemma. She was scheduled to sing that day. She wondered if she would be able to do it.

"What time do you have to be at the studio?" Rob inquired.

"Nine."

It was seven-thirty, and the studio was over an hour's drive from Paradise Cove.

"We'd better get a move on if you're going to be on time. But I'm wondering—are you going to be able to sing?"

"Maybe if I get enough fresh air on the way there, it'll clear up." She doubted her words as soon as she said them.

She dressed quickly as Rob made toast and coffee. As she applied her makeup, she fretted over her puffy eyes. Dammit! What could she do? Thank goodness they were recording and not shooting the video.

Before leaving, she threw her arms around Rob. He once again apologized profusely for Sagan. "I'll make it up to you tonight, my love. I'll take you out for a dinner you'll never forget."

"It's a deal." She gave him a final hasty kiss, knowing that she would barely have time to change clothes if she were to make it to the studio on time.

Once outside, she was greeted by the morning fog. She had no time to take much notice of it as she dashed to her car. She rummaged through her leather shoulder bag for the keys, cursing her inability to locate them—her purse was so disarranged.

Exasperated, she dug deeper, her fingers touching upon bottles of makeup, slick lipstick tubes, masses of wrinkled papers containing reminders and old credit card receipts, and other paraphernalia. But no keys.

She was prepared to dump the contents on the ground, when her eyes caught sight of the inside of her car. Her heart sank. There were her keys—hanging from the ignition! In her rush to get to Rob the previous evening, she must have left them there.

Frantically, she ran back to Rob's house and rang the bell. As he opened the door, the expression on his face was one of sheer surprise.

"Callie—what's wrong?"

"A hanger. I need a hanger."

"What are you talking about?"

"I locked my keys in the car. I'll have to break in."

"There's no time for that. Not if you're to get to the studio by nine. I'll drive you. I have to go to town anyway. It just means getting an earlier start. Really, Callie, it'll be fun." He gently ran his fingers along the contour of her face.

"Well, since you put it that way . . ." She met his sparkling eyes.

It could be like this every day, she thought as they began their journey along the Pacific Coast Highway. As they drove, the windows rolled down to allow for the damp morning air to enter, his hand rested gently upon hers.

They were traveling at a good pace until they got within three miles from the Sunset turnoff, the street leading to Callie's house. Suddenly, traffic came to a standstill.

They crept along sluggishly for several minutes, which felt like much longer, until they reached the road construction that was causing the congestion.

Callie glanced at her watch—it was nearly twenty after eight—and realized there was no way she would be able to change clothes. She was annoyed. Despite the blissful evening, the day was getting off to a bad start.

"There's no time to change." It was as if he had read her mind. "We can stop at your place before dinner and you can change then. That shouldn't be a problem, should it?"

"We have no choice. I'll probably be late as it is."

"Not if we don't hit any more traffic. Or at least you won't be too late." Rob consoled her, stroking her hand.

Miraculously, although traffic was heavy, it proceeded smoothly and they pulled in front of the studio only a few minutes after nine.

Although every moment counted, Callie couldn't resist giving Rob a final fiery kiss. After all, it would have to last her the rest of the day.

As she stepped out of the car, her eyes met a familiar face jeering at her—Tom Walden.

"Well, I'll be damned! If it isn't little Miss Prim-and-Proper herself. Dressed in the same outfit you had on yesterday, no less."

"So thoughtful of you to remember." Callie took large strides, intent on ignoring him.

"So that's it, huh? That's what all this whining has been about! Rob Matthews!"

She quickened her pace in her attempt to get away from him. But that didn't deter him. He kept on her heel, mimicking in a sarcastic voice, "Oh, no, I don't want to go on the road again. It's too soon. Oh, no, we should concentrate on what we're doing here. Oh, no . . ."

"Stop it, Tom. We're late. Or don't you care about that?"

"It seems to me that you're the one that doesn't care anymore, or at least not about anything having to do with Sizzle. Unless, of course, we're performing a Rob Matthews original."

"Just leave him out of this, Tom. I'm warning you—leave him out!"

"Or what, Callie? You'll quit the group?" Tom leered at her, his eyes radiating malice.

Could he know? No, it was impossible. Aghast, she nearly stopped in her tracks, but quickly regained her composure. "Come on. We don't have time to argue. We're running late, and time's important now." But she couldn't dismiss the thought that Tom might know about the audition for "Trinity Bluff." How could he possibly know?

"Sorry I'm running a bit late," Callie apologized as she hurried into the studio with Tom behind her.

"Yeah, she couldn't break away from Lover Boy and you'll never guess who the lucky guy happens to be."

"Please, Tom." Callie threw him a pleading look, but it was to no avail.

"Rob Matthews! *The* Rob Matthews no less!"

So, there. It was out! She felt a heated flush beginning to form, but then something inside of her snapped. So what if people knew—it was true. Suddenly, she didn't care who knew—let the whole world know—she and Rob Matthews were in love!

Vic quickly changed the subject, insisting they get down to business.

When Callie got her cue, she opened her mouth, but instead of her usual smooth soprano, her voice sounded raspy and uneven. She cracked on the high notes, and sounded more like a scratched record than a professional singer.

She panicked! My God! She had forgotten about Sagan and her allergy attack. The fresh air on the drive in had done nothing to alleviate her condition. Furthermore, the long cat hairs on her sweater were adding to her discomfort.

Vic had the band cut the number. "What are we going to do? We can't record this with your voice like that!"

What was she to do? The damage had already been done. She refused Lynne's offer of nasal spray as well as Ken's suggestion to run out for some allergy medication, knowing it would be to no avail. It was obvious that she would not be able to sing that day. While she picked the cat hairs from her sweater, the other members of the group made no attempt to disguise their annoyance.

"Just what we needed—a wasted day!" Tom sent accusatory looks in her direction.

"Now. Now." Vic attempted to calm them. "It won't be entirely wasted. We needed to go over those takes of the video, so now we can do that."

"It's just a big waste of time for us to be here." Guy sulked. "You don't need us to do that."

"It wouldn't hurt for the rest of you to see them."

"It wouldn't hurt for Callie to take care of herself at a critical time like this," Tom returned.

"It wasn't my fault. I couldn't help it."

But it was no use. As they shuffled out the door, it was obvious to Callie that everyone was upset with her.

"Oh, Vic, I'm sorry," Callie said, sighing, when the last member of the group had left the studio. "But it wasn't as if I did this on purpose."

"I know that, Callie. But I don't have to tell you how uptight everyone's been lately."

"I know. No word from Electric yet, huh?"

"No word. But let's not think about that now. Let's take a look at this tape and see if there're any changes we need to make."

Vic pushed the On button and Callie observed herself singing "Has Gotta Be Real." Before long they realized it was the original take they were watching, not the one with the changes she and Rob had agreed upon.

"Sorry." Vic changed tapes.

"Too bad we can't use the first version," Callie said. "I like it better than the remake."

"Well, I don't think it would be a good idea," Vic remarked. "Especially now." He gave her a knowing look.

"Especially now," Callie emphasized.

Vic and Callie spent an hour reviewing the tape. The only interruption was a phone call from Rob confirming the time he was to meet her at the studio. After a brief lunch break, they finished their critique of the videotape and went on to look over possible photos for the album cover.

By four they were both tired, and Vic suggested they call it a day. Callie told him she wanted to look at the video a few more times before giving it final approval. Anyway, she needed to be at the studio to meet Rob. Once she was alone after Vic left, she hugged herself thinking of the romantic evening that lay ahead.

When Rob appeared, punctual as always, she threw her arms around him. It was as if she hadn't seen him for days rather than hours. As he held her, she felt the tensions melting away. She snuggled closer, wishing she could always remain in the serene security of his embrace.

"Don't worry, my love. Everything will be fine in the morning. You just wait and see."

As their lips met, she hoped his words would come true.

Chapter Ten
❖ ❖ ❖

EARLY THE NEXT morning Callie entered the studio to a stifling silence. She looked around at the sullen faces. Surely the group couldn't still be angry about the previous day?

"So where are they?" Tom said, accusingly.

"What are you talking about?"

"The tapes. The tapes that you reviewed yesterday. They've disappeared!"

"What!" Callie was incredulous.

"I'm sorry to say it's true," Vic confirmed. "They appear to have been misplaced. We were hoping you'd know where they are."

"But I don't understand. They've got to be here. I locked the door when I left."

But was she sure? Could she have been so engrossed in Rob, so anxious to be in his arms again that she could have forgotten to lock the door? But even if she had forgotten, Callie reasoned to herself, why would anyone want the tapes?

"This is just great." Tom made no attempt to hide his bitter sarcasm. "We're on a deadline, it looks as if our contract isn't going to be renewed—"

"So let's stop this infighting," Vic interrupted, "and try to get ourselves together. I'm sure Callie wouldn't intentionally lose those tapes. Think hard, Callie. Try to recreate what happened after I left you."

It wasn't difficult to bring back the image of Rob, to remember the tingle his touch had created as he listened to her woeful day. But her memory blurred as she attempted to recall locking the door when they left.

Still, the question haunted her—what would anyone want with the tapes? Sure, people pirated tapes of Bob Dylan and The Beatles and later released them underground for phenomenal prices, but she'd be flattering herself to think that Sizzle was popular enough for anyone to try to bootleg. Further, she doubted that a stranger could get past the security guards in the lobby.

"There's got to be an explanation," Callie thought aloud.

"Look who's doing the wishful thinking today," Tom challenged.

"All the wishful thinking in the world isn't going to get this album done," Vic interceded. "Greg's following up on the tapes, so it's time for us to get to work."

It was difficult but necessary for Callie to dismiss the silent accusations of the band. In view of the time they had lost the previous day, she forced herself to concentrate on her performance.

The other members of the group, however, were not as cooperative. They fumbled on one thing or another, making several retakes necessary. It was almost as if they were intentionally making mistakes to punish her.

Dammit! Was she getting paranoid? She managed to maintain her concentration despite the numerous retakes and disgruntled comments that were mumbled around her.

After the fourth take of "Stormy Dreams," she was happy to receive a call on the studio phone. Expecting it to be Rob, she was surprised to hear a woman's voice instead.

"I hope you don't mind me calling there, but this is urgent! Sharon gave me the number when I told her how important it was."

It was Vicki Blake, the agent Sharon had recommended. Before Callie could respond, Vicki continued. "I think they're really interested in you for 'Trinity Bluff,' but there're complications. They've just canned the old director and hired some new hotshot. He wants to see you. Pronto."

"Do you mean today?"

"Sooner if possible."

"It's impossible—I can't get away!"

"Well, I think you're making a mistake, but if you really can't swing it, I'll think of something to stall them. I'm sure we can't put them off any later than tomorrow."

As Callie made hurried arrangements to meet with the new director the next day, Greg, the assistant producer, entered the studio triumphantly waving two videotapes. She was grateful that they had been found, relieving her of at least one worry.

"You know this happens all the time." Greg shrugged his shoulders as he presented the tapes to Vic.

"Yes, I know," Vic confirmed. "Believe me, I know only too well!"

While no one bothered to apologize to her, the group's performance indicated their much-improved mood. Though Callie was grateful that the tapes had been located, she still felt uneasy about the unjust accusations from the band.

When Rob called later that evening, she told him about the latest development with "Trinity Bluff." She didn't mention the incident with the tapes, however, because she knew he was under a lot of pressure to complete the film score for Lance Eddenberg.

But the truth was that the band's rejection hurt. Still, now I have to concentrate on "Trinity Bluff," she told herself as she sat in the reception room, studying her lines for the show's new director.

However, as she studied the script she realized that she wasn't the only person in the room concentrating on her part. Two other women as young as herself were seated in opposing corners intently submerged in what was obviously the same script. Neither of them looked up, but the tension in the room was thick.

Callie furtively studied the other two candidates. Hadn't Vicki implied she all but had the part? So what were these other women doing there?

She turned her attention back to the script, and a few minutes later yet another young, shapely blonde entered. The newcomer looked familiar to Callie, someone she had seen around town, hanging out at all the "in" places, but she couldn't recall her name.

"Callie Stevens! I can hardly believe it!"

Callie wished the plush beige couch would swallow her up. Not only had she totally forgotten the other woman's name, but she also became aware that the two other women, who had up until that time ignored her, were staring at her openly.

"I know," the intruder continued, "you don't remember. Clyde Thomas's party—you were with Nick Steward—remember now?"

"I'm—"

"Of course. You must have been so engrossed with Nicky that all us little people faded into the wall. I'm Lauren Banks, but my friends all call me Laurie."

"Well, it's been such a long time," Callie said apologetically as she futilely attempted to meet Lauren's eyes, which were busily scanning the room. Lauren Banks, she recalled, had a reputation for gaining roles through her friendships with key people rather than by her talent. It was difficult to believe that she was up for the lead on "Trinity Bluff."

"Oh, by the way"—Laurie lowered her voice, still peering around the room with her heavily shadowed eyes—"I'm really sorry about Sizzle looking for a new female lead. That's probably why you're here, right?"

Sizzle replacing her! Was it possible? That explained a lot. No wonder they had been so hard on her lately.

"Uhm, well, ah . . ." Callie mumbled, hoping her shock wasn't apparent. She was relieved when Ellen Falk abruptly entered, shadowed by an attractive older man, putting an end to the disturbing conversation.

Lauren sprang to her feet, directing her attention to the man at Ellen's side.

"David, darling!" She threw herself into his arms.

He graciously returned her kiss. Assuming this was David Templeton, the new director, Callie viewed the impassioned scene with apprehension.

"Excuse me," Ellen interjected, clearing her throat. Lauren slowly pulled away from David as Ellen continued. "Ms. Stevens has to be back at the studio, and I promised her agent we'd get her in and out as quickly as possible."

Callie felt her palms sweating as she followed Ellen. She wondered about what Lauren had said. Was the group really looking to replace her? Or was it just a clever way to psych her out and make her blow the interview?

As she entered the studio, Ellen formally introduced her to David Templeton.

"So, we finally meet." The director shot her a noncommittal smile as he clutched her fingers with his strong tan hand.

Callie noticed his eyes were a deep green and his hair was slightly graying around the temples. A good-looking man, she assessed. No wonder all the starlets threw themselves at him. Well, she certainly hoped he didn't expect the same type of behavior from her.

"You're even more beautiful in person than on your album covers, and I had no idea that you have such a terrific body!"

Stunned, she was speechless, but her face suffused with heat.

"Please. Don't get offended. I made that comment only to see if you blush."

"Are you satisfied now?"

"Very."

Callie met his eyes, searching for a message, but was unable to find one.

"Well, so much for the preliminaries. What do you say we get down to business?"

Callie's hands trembled slightly as she read the lines. How she wished she hadn't been distracted by that stupid woman in the reception room! Still, she managed to throw herself into the reading. After a few lines it was as if nothing disturbing had occurred.

"Okay—cut!" David interrupted, his deep neutral voice surprising her mid-sentence. "That'll be all."

"But I've just begun—"

"That's okay. I've heard enough."

Enough? *You haven't given me a chance,* she wanted to cry out, but held herself back. She knew enough about the business to know that it was foolish to try to argue with the director. It could only alienate him. But this was highly unusual and she couldn't imagine why he wasn't giving her the opportunity to complete the scene.

"Thank you so much for coming at such short notice," Ellen Falk commented in her businesslike voice, her dark eyes darting over her oversize glasses. She, too, was not giving Callie any clues as to how the audition had gone.

"Yes, thank you." As he said the words, he jotted something down in his notebook.

"Thank you for giving me the chance to audition." Callie kept her voice calm in spite of her feelings. She unsuccessfully attempted to make eye contact with Templeton again.

As she quickly made her way out of the office, she intentionally avoided Lauren Banks. She nearly dropped her handbag in her attempt to play it cool.

My God, this director was even less responsive than the previous one! Callie had no idea how he had felt about her reading. And the presence of Lauren Banks and the other women in the reception area hardly inspired confidence.

She relived the scene, but it became foggier rather than clearer. As she drove back to the recording studio, her apprehension escalated.

By the time Callie reentered the studio, she was in no mood for bad news. Sizzle's contract had not been renewed, and Vic hadn't been able to sign them with another label. At least not yet. Callie felt miserable, and luck would have it that Rob would be working again that evening with Lance Eddenberg. Dammit, she sure needed a strong shoulder to cry on!

Everyone was glum during the session, yet aware of the limited studio time, so they appeared willing to make the most of it. Cooperation was at an all-time peak, and things went smoothly in spite of the gloom.

"Can I talk with you a moment?" Callie approached Vic when the session was over.

"Sure. You know I always have time for you, Callie."

Callie sensed real warmth in his words. Despite his occasional off-beat jibing, he had always been supportive of her. She knew she could trust him.

As she approached his office, she wasn't quite sure how she was going to bring up the subject, but once they were alone, she immediately blurted out what Lauren Banks had told her that day.

"Oh, that! I'm surprised you haven't heard about that sooner!"

Callie stayed rooted to her spot, stunned. Then there was something to the rumor! Conflicting feelings flooded her. Maybe it was good that they were already seeking a replacement for her. But what if she didn't get the part on "Trinity Bluff"? And she still was ambivalent about leaving the band!

"Look, you know how difficult Tom can be. Well, it seems that he has this new girlfriend—Chicky. She's a fairly decent singer—can't hold a candle to you, but she's not bad. Anyway, it seems that he has this crazy notion to train her for the lead."

"But what about the other members of the group—how did they feel about this?"

"Do you even have to ask? They were against it, of course. Especially Ken.

"But Tom's been real pigheaded about it." Vic shook his head and shrugged his shoulders. "You know how things can go hot and cold. Heaven knows, I've been in this business long enough to see stranger things. And, of course, I opposed it from the start."

"I believe that, Vic."

She knew that Vic was on her side, and was relieved to know that it was only Tom who had suggested replacing her. Still, things had changed. Maybe it was time for her to move on. Maybe it would be best for everyone involved.

"So what's the next move?" Callie inquired.

"Probably going back on the road. It looks as if we have no other prospects at this time. I hate to say it, but I think we're going to have to think seriously about a major tour—and soon."

The dryness in her throat made it difficult to answer. She wished she could tell him about "Trinity Bluff," but she really didn't know what there was to tell him. Instead, she merely sighed as she acknowledged, "Yes, that's what I was afraid of."

"Look, Callie, I know how you feel about that. To tell you the truth, I'm not exactly keen on the idea myself. Margaret is even less enthusiastic, so I can imagine how things must be with you . . ."

He didn't have to complete the sentence. Things were out in the open about her and Rob. She wondered if he knew how instrumental he had been getting the two of them back together. She had felt like telling him a number of times, but the appropriate moment had never arrived.

Callie knew that he and his wife Margaret had had difficulties because of his traveling. Like Rob, Margaret was a family person and holidays like Thanksgiving and Christmas meant a lot to her. How difficult this past holiday season must have been for her and the children with Vic away on tour. If Vic became her personal manager, Callie reasoned, all this could change for him as well.

"I don't know," she mused, pushing curly locks of hair away from her face. "Sometimes I think it would be better if I left the group."

Relief spread through her as she voiced her feelings aloud.

Vic squirmed in his seat. "Are you sure that's what you really want? We all have doubts about what we're doing at times. Believe me, I know how you feel about going on the road again. But are you sure you are not reacting emotionally to Tom's rebuff? You know, I don't know what's going on between the two of you, but I'd be willing to bet it has something to do with the West Coast tour."

"You'd have a good bet there."

"Okay. So the two of you aren't seeing eye-to-eye now. These things happen. These things also pass, you know. If I were you, I wouldn't do anything rash or let some outlandish rumors influence you." Vic looked at her steadily.

"It's not just that," Callie confessed. How she wished that she could tell him everything. But she couldn't. She knew it would be better to wait and see what happened with "Trinity Bluff" first.

"Listen, don't take it so hard," Vic continued. "Things may change. Who knows, maybe some other company will sign us up."

As he said the words, Callie knew he didn't believe them any more than she did. At least, she doubted that another company would sign them for a while. She knew that a major road trip was necessary to generate publicity.

And yet, as she walked into her house that evening, she found herself deep in thought about her situation. If she got the part on "Trinity Bluff," Chicky could replace her in Sizzle and go on the road and she could stay in Los Angeles with Rob and never have to deal with being on the road again. But what if she didn't get the part?

She glanced around her living room, noting how its underdecorated starkness contrasted with the thoughtfully decorated rooms in Rob's house. Her polished hardwood floors seemed naked without rugs; her few Brian Davis prints barely compensated for the overabundance of blank wall space. Even the pale mauve couch lacked warmth.

This was definitely a room not lived in—a room typical of someone who was rarely there. Someone who didn't really live in a *home.* How fed up she was with her present lifestyle! But still, she could never abandon her career, give up everything she had worked so hard for for all these years.

Later, as she soaked in a steamy bubble bath, things about her place began to stand out in alarming detail. God, whatever had possessed her to do her bathroom in red? She had had a decorator do her place, and it was obvious. Nothing about this house reflected her own personality. Somehow, recalling Rob's tan sunken tub and the pale tones of beige and aqua that complemented each other, the feelings she had while leisurely bathing there also came back to her.

She recalled her conversation with Vic, how relieved she had felt when she voiced her feelings aloud.

"Yes, I'm ready for a change," she softly voiced to the brightly patterned wallpaper, and a wave of complete calm came over her.

But she knew, as Vic had pointed out, that this was much too big a decision to make rashly. *And if she were to leave Sizzle?* Regardless of the outcome of the television role, she knew she must leave on a positive note. She was a professional, and she owed that to herself and to the group.

As she inhaled the fresh magnolia scent of her powder, she wished she could call Rob and hear the soft reassurance of his voice. She longed for him to tell her of his love, to let her know that what really mattered the most to her was still intact. But she dared not interrupt when he was working with Lance Eddenberg. He told her he would call when he could—she would just have to be content with the memory of him holding her in his arms.

She went to her bedroom with hopes that the soft shades of pink and lavender would soothe her, but was met by a wild disarray of scattered outfits, unpaired shoes, perfumes, eyeliners, and other odds and ends.

Ignoring the clutter, she roamed over to her jewelry box. She touched the necklace Rob had given her—the G-clef pendant with the rubies. She hadn't worn it since the night he had first given it to her because it reminded her of the stormy argument that evening.

But suddenly, as she clasped the charm to her, she realized that she was in control. Whether she got the part on "Trinity Bluff" or not, she would survive. There would be other television roles, or other groups, or she could go out on her own and be like Madonna or Whitney Houston. But deep in her heart she knew that in Rob she had found her true match.

The telephone startled her. She grabbed it, hoping it would be Rob.

"I miss you . . ." His voice was soothing.

"I miss you too. So much."

"Just hearing your voice makes me want to hold you close and never let you go."

"Is that a comment or a request?"

"I'm afraid it's only wishful thinking tonight, my love. Lance just left, and things are frantic. They're recording the sound score tomorrow and there're still major changes I need to make. I'll be tied up well into the wee hours of the morning, much as I'd rather be kept busy in a more romantic manner."

She sighed. "I understand."

She did, but of course would much rather have been with him. She wanted to tell him about the recent developments, but how could she burden him when he was under pressure to meet a deadline? Perhaps the old Callie Stevens might have blurted out the news without hesitation, but she knew she could wait for a more appropriate time.

"Darling, is anything wrong?" His voice was filled with concern.

Was he that close to her that he was able to tell that something had happened just from the tone of her voice?

"Well, I miss you. Other than that, things haven't changed that much." She fibbed to keep him from worrying. "It's been a long day, that's all."

"And we sure didn't get much sleep the other night, did we?" he teased her.

"Oh, are you complaining?"

"Are you kidding!"

The silence that followed brought memories of the last evening they had spent together. Her senses stirred from just the thought of the way they had kissed, the way he had looked into her eyes and declared his love, the way she had felt so serene in the strength of his arms.

"Seriously, my love, I should have this score completed by early afternoon tomorrow. Then I just have to run it into Lance in Hollywood and I could be over to get you at the studio in time for dinner—we'll celebrate."

How grateful she was that he would have something to celebrate. She hoped she might have some good news for him as well.

"Sounds wonderful."

"I'll call if there're any complications, but there shouldn't be. I miss you."

"Mmmm . . ."

"Now, don't start that purring. You know I can't resist you when you do that."

"Even over the telephone?"

"Even over the telephone! Good night, Callie, and sweet dreams."

As she placed the receiver down and glanced around her disorderly room, she doubted that she would be having any kind of dreams that night.

Chapter Eleven
❖ ❖ ❖

WHEN CALLIE ENTERED the studio the next day, her thoughts were as well organized as the pile of clothes she had sorted the previous evening. The question was no longer if she wanted to leave the group, but how and when to announce her decision. Not now, she knew. The last sessions were crucial. The group's future depended on their outcome. They had to be good! And she certainly owed Sizzle her best effort.

In the interest of group harmony, she pushed aside her misgivings about Tom. She ignored the wisecracks and jeering smiles he would intermittently throw her. She swallowed her pride and smiled evenly in return.

"Good going!" Vic cried out when they finished the number. "If we keep it up, we should have this song down today. We might make our deadline yet!"

"We'd better." Lynne let her electric guitar fall to her side and shrugged her shoulders. "I still can't believe Electric is making us record two extra numbers after not renewing our contract!"

"They still want to sell albums, you know. Besides, it's not so unusual for a company to reject a song or two now and then."

"Yeah, but it makes it even harder when you're running out of time." Guy angrily plucked a string on his bass guitar for emphasis.

Suddenly, Greg called out across the crowded studio, "Phone call for Callie."

Could it be Rob with a change of plans? The thought flashed through her mind as she raced to the phone. The spike heels that matched her pale lilac dress clicked as she raced across the room.

The outfit she had deliberated upon for so long the night before was intentionally understated. Somehow her old standbys didn't seem right. She rejected the bright fuchsias and reds in favor of the soft light knit dress that clung to her shapely contours. She hoped Rob would approve.

When she answered the phone, a man's deep voice, vaguely familiar, came on. "Hello, Ms. Stevens. This is David Templeton. I need to see you right away."

"Today? I'm afraid that's not possible."

"It's rather urgent." His voice became bolder.

In Hollywood, Callie reflected, everything was urgent. Nothing existed unless it was a crisis. However, she could hardly refuse the invitation—he was the director and she wanted the part.

"Well, all right, but I don't have much time."

"That's all right. This shouldn't take long."

What could he mean by that? Callie mused on her way over to the restaurant David had suggested. This was one of the new places on La Cienega where the size of the portions was inversely related to the prices, but the ambiance was as smooth as the wine she sat slowly sipping. David was waiting for her when she got there and escorted her to a table in the back garden.

"Why don't you take those sunglasses off," David said brusquely as soon as he arrived. "I find them terribly distracting. When I talk to someone, I like to look in their eyes. Or are you trying not to be recognized?"

"No, it's not that," Callie assured him, although she was feeling self-conscious about the stares she was getting from the "celebrity watchers." "It's just the sun's rather bright today."

"We could eat inside if you'd like, but I rather think it's nice out here. Where I'm from, you could never dine outside in December."

"Oh, where's that?"

"New York City. How about you?"

"I'm a native Californian. Graduated from Venice High, class of 'seventy-six."

"Did you go to college out here too? Or did you join up with Sizzle immediately after high school?"

"I graduated in theater arts at UCLA and became the lead in Sizzle right after that. But I've done television in the past, and acting was always my first love."

Considering the fact that everything he had

asked her was stated on her résumé, she doubted that he was concerned about her professional abilities. The way his emerald eyes held hers convinced her that he had something other than small talk on his mind. But how could she get him to come to the point?

"Relax. I'm not here to quiz you." David gave her a wide, close-mouthed smile, his eyes gleaming as the sun's rays fell upon them.

She wanted to ask why he had asked her there —what the urgency was—but before she could say anything, a waiter approached.

"Nice to see you again, Mr. Templeton."

"Thank you, Scotty."

Scotty directed his attention to Callie, who had not had a chance to examine the menu.

She skimmed over the ornate calligraphy, spotting an entree called Brochette Olivia, whose description vaguely resembled a hamburger.

"And how would madame like that prepared?"

She had to stop herself from saying "cooked," as she mumbled "medium" to him.

David ordered a spinach salad.

"Amazing how you young people can eat anything you like." He grinned. "But after thirty, things change."

Surely he hadn't invited her here to discuss her age or diet. What could she say to make him get to the point?

"My youngest sister just turned thirty," he continued, "and almost overnight she's had to watch what she eats. Lord knows, I miss her, and my kids from my first marriage. They're all back east still. Now I have only two golden retrievers to keep me company."

Oh, no, the old come-on, she mused, but said nothing. She decided she'd let him play his hand.

He paused, and almost as if he had read her mind, continued. "But I didn't invite you here to talk about me. I want to know about you. Tell me, do you have any brothers or sisters?"

"No, I'm an only child." For goodness' sake, where was that waiter already?

"Were your parents in the entertainment business?"

"No, my mother taught third grade. She's remarried now and lives in Florida. I haven't seen my father since junior high."

"Oh, I'm sorry. That must have been hard—growing up without a father."

"Well, it's not so uncommon, you know." Callie felt defensive despite attempts to remain calm.

"That's what I thought when my wife and I broke up. It may be common, but it still hurt like hell."

It was all coming back to her. She felt a wave of sorrow as she recalled the pain of her past—the trauma of her father's final departure, the anguished tears her mother tried to hide from her, and the bitter hurt she felt.

Blinking back tears, she pursed her lips and indignantly proclaimed, "I really don't see what this has to do with the part in 'Trinity Bluff'!"

"It has plenty to do with it!" His hands flew into the air, adding emphasis to his words. "Congratulations—you just got it!"

She just got it! She got the part! An exuberant rush surged through her veins. She remained speechless, stunned by the roller coaster of emotions David had just taken her on.

"You see," he went on to explain, "I just did a little exercise with you to see if you could readily put yourself into another emotional frame of mind. You passed with flying colors!"

"When do I start?" was all she could say despite her unsettled emotions.

"Not for several weeks. Ellen Falk will get in touch with your agent. They'll arrange everything. I was ninety-nine percent sold the minute you read the first line. But I couldn't resist this final little audition. Plus, I wanted to tell you the news myself." He gave her a smile and met her eyes. "I think we're going to work well together."

His confident smile and steady eyes gave credence to the words. "I think so too," she answered honestly.

The waiter returned and placed a plate with a small hamburger on it in front of her. Callie gazed at it and then her watch.

"Oh, my God! It's late. I've got to get back to the studio."

"But your lunch . . ."

"Give it to your dogs. I'm sure they'll like it! I can't think of food at a time like this—I'm too happy!"

"That's one way to stay slim." David waved her off with his warm smile.

She floated to her car. Walking would have been too slow, too close to the ground for the way she was feeling. If only she could call Rob to share the good news! But she had no idea where he might be at the movie studio. Besides, she wanted to tell him in person. She fantasized how his face would glow when she told him and how he would swing her in his arms with joy.

As she bounced from the parking lot into the studio, she couldn't help but notice that everything appeared so alive. The sky looked lighter, the azure blue almost dancing with sunbeams. The hazy hills added a fairytale-like touch to the picture.

"Well, look who's here, Tinker Bell. If you beamed any more, you probably would fly." Tom again.

"Oh, am I late? I'm sorry, I thought—"

"No, you're not late," Vic assured her. "The engineers aren't due back until two."

Oh, how she wished she could tell Vic the good news right there and then. She was going to ask him to be her manager. Greg could take over with Sizzle. Being young and single, he would relish the travel.

No more road tours! A major part in a prime-time television show! Never having to be away from Rob again! Callie could hardly believe her incredible luck. Everything was coming together for her more perfectly than she ever could have planned it.

"You all did great today!" Vic said with animation as the session ended three hours later. "Especially you, Callie." Callie smiled; her voice must have reflected her joy.

As the group disassembled a little after six, Vic approached Callie. "You haven't been over to the house in a while. How'd you like to join Margaret and the kids and me for dinner?"

"Oh, I'd love to. But let's make it some other time, Vic. Rob's completing a sound score today and we're going to go out to celebrate. He should be here any minute."

Actually, Rob should have been there several minutes ago, but rush hour traffic was always unpredictable. Or perhaps he had a few last-minute things to go over with Lance Eddenberg. At any rate, she felt confident that he'd be there soon.

However, half an hour later, when Rob had still not shown up, her confidence began to wane. It was so unlike him to be late. Callie flitted around the empty studio, finding it difficult to contain her excitement about getting the part. She was eager to share her news, and her enthusiasm made the time crawl.

By six forty-five she became worried. Could something have happened to him? She called the movie studio, but when the switchboard operator connected her with Lance Eddenberg's office, there was no answer.

This was not like Rob. He would have called her if he was going to be detained. Where could he be?

At seven-fifteen she tried the studio again, but there was still no answer. She was antsy. She could stand it no longer. She couldn't wait around the empty studio for him—it was just too nerve-wracking. She scribbled a note saying that she had gone home and taped it to the door.

Not unlike her mood, the weather had changed from a warm, wonderful day to a nasty night. A harsh Santa Ana wind was gusting through the now dim streets, sending unsettling undercurrents swirling through the previously calm day.

She drove to her home in the Hollywood Hills, but being in an empty house was no solace; it just aggravated her need to share her news. At the same time, Rob's unexplainable absence gnawed upon her every nerve. Where was he anyway? Could he have forgotten?

She tried calling his house, but there was no answer. And, of course, Lance Eddenberg's telephone number was unlisted. What could she do? She would burst if she couldn't tell somebody about getting the part on "Trinity Bluff."

She called Sharon, who convinced her to come over. Some annoyance had already filtered in with her concern, and as she scribbled yet another note to Rob, she was already feeling angry.

"Well, there must be an explanation," Sharon insisted as Callie gobbled a handful of chips. "You're overreacting because you were so keyed up to tell him the news about 'Trinity Bluff.'"

"Yeah. I guess you're right." Callie shrugged her shoulders, unable to hide her disappointment.

She glanced around the room. This was one of the quieter moments at Sharon's house. The kids were bathed and tucked into bed, and although Doug was working late, the room didn't appear empty. Photographs of the four of them were abundant—several framed ones on one wall, a multiple-photograph holder on the coffee table, and photograph albums were stacked on a shelf of the nearby bookshelves. The presence of a colorful push toy and scattered wooden blocks served as reminders of the day's activities.

"It's nice . . ." Callie mumbled aloud.

"What's nice?"

"This room. The way it feels so . . . comfortable and lived-in."

"If that's what you think, you've changed more than I ever would have imagined."

Callie lowered her head but said nothing. Her blond curls fell into her face as she took in the silence of the evening. All that could be heard was the sound of the powerful Santa Ana wind roaring outside the room.

She grabbed another handful of potato chips and poured herself a glass of soda.

"You're sure eating a lot of junk for someone who isn't hungry. Why don't you at least let me make you a sandwich."

"I'm eating out," Callie insisted as she munched on the chips. She had refused Sharon's previous offer of dinner, expecting Rob to show up at any minute. But it was already after nine o'clock. Now the question was if he was going to show up at all. She was beginning to doubt it.

"Look, I know you're upset about Rob, and I don't blame you. But you're supposed to be celebrating."

"Tell me about it," Callie said on a sigh. She was

concerned, confused, and disappointed all at once.

Darting nervously toward the telephone, Callie grabbed it and dialed his number again, allowing it to ring at least twenty times before hanging up.

"Dammit! I wish he had an answering machine or service like normal people!" She sighed and continued. "Besides, this wind is driving me crazy! If I don't do something, I'm going to go out of my mind."

"There's really nothing you can do," Sharon observed.

Just then Callie heard someone approach the front door. Could it be Rob? But when the door opened and Doug stepped in, she became again aware of the gnawing hollowness at the pit of her stomach.

"Hey, Callie!" Doug gave her an affectionate bear hug appropriate for the "teddy bear" that he was. Doug was stocky, and his prematurely bald head made him appear older than his thirty-four years, but he was a warm and gentle man. A perfect husband for Sharon. When he released her, he observed, "But you look awful! Have you been working too hard?"

"Ha! You should talk." Sharon snuggled up to him and planted a big kiss on his bald head before explaining what was going on.

"Oh, Callie, you know how these things go. When you're working in the studio, you can completely lose track of time."

"But he was finished working," Callie insisted. "He only had to run the score over to Lance. Besides, even if he was detained, surely he would have called me. It just isn't like Rob to be this inconsiderate."

"I've asked her to spend the night here," Sharon informed Doug.

"You might as well," Doug encouraged. "After all, there's really nothing you can do."

"Oh, yes, there is!" Suddenly, the idea hit her. Callie grabbed her coat and purse as she announced, "I'm going to go to his house!"

"Well, drive carefully." Sharon looked worried as she hugged her good-bye.

"Stop worrying—I'll be fine. If I don't go there, I'll go batty."

Determination set in as she stepped out into the dry, gusting wind. First she would stop at her house and check her answering machine for messages. Maybe Rob had called. Quickly, she made her way through the familiar curving roads of the Hollywood Hills. She dashed up the steps leading to her front door. The note she had left for Rob was gone! If he had gotten the note, why hadn't he gone to Sharon's house?

"I hate bothering you again, Sharon," Callie panted into the phone. "But the note I left Rob was gone, so I thought we might have crossed paths as I was coming home."

But her hopes were short-lived. Sharon told her that Rob wasn't there.

Now, truly baffled, she raced to her answering machine. The red light was flashing, but the message was not the one she wanted to hear. "Hi, Callie. This is Vicki. Congratulations on the part! I knew we could do it! I'm going over some of the details on your contract and will have it ready within a few days. Give me a call at your convenience and we'll set up a time for you to sign it."

The message was followed by two hang-ups which Callie knew weren't Rob. As much as he disliked answering machines, he always left word when he called.

She dialed his number. Once again, no answer. As she headed out the door, she didn't question what she was hoping to accomplish by her mission—she just knew she had to do something.

The haunting and ominous wind increased as she drove the long stretch of highway that led to Rob's house. Her nerves were frazzled and unsteady from the exhaustion of the long, eventful day. She grasped the steering wheel with both hands, hoping her measure of caution would make up for her impulsive decision.

When she arrived, everything was dark and still with the exception of the bawling wind. She rang the bell several times, but there was no answer. She debated using the spare key. When Rob had shown her where it was hidden, adding, "just in case you should ever need it," she'd doubted that she would. She certainly couldn't stand outside on the stoop all night, especially with this crazy wind howling. Giving in, she reached for the key, her heart thudding as she slipped it into the lock.

Feeling like a trespasser, she tiptoed from room to room in the darkness. Working her way along the living room, her fingers grazed the luscious leather couch as she inched her way along in the dark. She made her way down the hallway leading to Rob's bedroom, still feeling too reluctant to switch on the light.

As she stepped into his bedroom, her eyes were becoming accustomed to the darkness. She inhaled the familiar lime scent but heard nothing. She made her way to his studio, hoping to discover a clue to his whereabouts there.

It was too dark to see anything inside the windowless room. Suddenly, as she flicked on the light, she heard a crash! She jumped back, her eyes darting around the room. She caught sight of the music stand that had just fallen to the floor. Next to it emerged two chartreuse eyes. Then the surprised feline dashed past her out the door.

Callie put the music stand back in place, noting the disarranged condition of the room. It was unlike Rob to allow this room in particular to become so disorderly. It was obvious that he must have been working long hours and hadn't bothered taking the time to clean up when he had finished.

But she already knew how hard he had been working, and as she glanced at the various papers that filled the area, she noted that they were all filled with musical notes and notations to accompany the film he was scoring. But there were no clues as to where he could be at that moment and why he had not met her at the studio. As a last resort she checked the garage.

Before leaving, she debated whether she should write a note, but decided against it. What was the point? Besides, what would she say? Her anger was now getting the best of her.

The wind buffeted her Mercedes, demanding that she pay added attention to the road as she drove the long and curving road back to her house. The demands of the highway temporarily occupied her mind, diverting her attention away from her irritation with Rob.

By the time she arrived at her house, it was already past eleven o'clock. She called Rob's number once again; there was no answer.

An eerie sensation overtook her, as if she were not alone. She heard a rustling sound coming from somewhere inside her house. She anxiously pursued the noise to its source—a room in the far end that was intended to be used as her office. As she entered, a blast of air chilled her face. The Santa Ana must have forced the window open. She looked in dismay at the havoc the powerful wind had created. Scattered around her were old fan letters, lead sheets, magazine articles, and other material she had never gotten around to filing.

Disgusted, she closed the window, shutting out the ghostly, howling cries. As she made a futile attempt to collect some of the papers, it dawned on her—of course, why hadn't she thought of it before—the note she had left for Rob on her front door had probably met the same fate the papers that lay scattered around the room did! But what about the note at the studio? Surely it had not been affected by the Santa Ana!

She paced her hardwood floors. Time crept as her mind raced through various possibilities.

She was too tense to eat and too jumpy to take a bath. Finally, convinced she wouldn't be seeing Rob that evening, she changed into a faded flannel nightgown. But she couldn't stay in bed. She dialed Rob's number again. And again. But she never got an answer.

This was all so unreal. She just couldn't believe it. This was a night they should be out celebrating, but instead she was alone in her empty house with no idea where Rob could be. Only the roaring wind, shaking the plate glass windows and sobbing in the night, was there to keep her company.

Chapter Twelve
❖❖❖

AFTER BEING SWEPT clean by last night's ferocious winds, the city glistened. Even the nearby mountains, usually obstructed by smog, were visible as Callie headed down the hills the next morning. The serenity of the scene was at odds with her mood, and the breathtaking views did little to uplift her sullen spirits.

Still unable to reach Rob that morning, she

didn't know what to think. Had he stood her up? Or had something happened to him?

As she pulled onto Sunset Boulevard, a news item on the car radio caught her attention: "Due to unusually powerful winds last night, telephone lines are down in parts of Los Angeles and Malibu . . ."

Telephone lines down! Was that why she had been unable to reach Rob? Still, where had he been when he was supposed to have met her at the studio? Why hadn't he gone to her house? With these and other unresolved questions plaguing her, she was hardly in the mood for the news that awaited her as she entered the studio.

"Wait'll you see this!" Guy called out, extending a magazine in her direction.

Callie gasped at the sight that met her eyes. There, in black and white on cheap newsprint, a picture jumped out at her. It was of Tom and her in a seemingly rapturous embrace.

Suddenly it all came back to her—San Francisco—the Hyatt Regency—flashbulbs popping as Tom unsuccessfully attempted to kiss her while the rude photographer from *Pop Star* refused to be deterred. So that explained the smirking looks Tom was throwing her yesterday.

"Way to go Callie! We needed some publicity!" Lynne joined in.

"Yeah, and this reporter had a lot of good things to say about the tour. It's nice to have a friend in a magazine like *Pop Star* at a time like this," Guy added. The other members of the band were oblivious to her irritation. They thought any type of publicity was good!

She didn't know whom to be angrier at—Tom or the photographer. But what good was it? The harm had already been done.

"Not a bad picture, huh?" Tom baited her.

"Even if it's not true." She pursed her lips and kept her voice steady but made no attempt to conceal the icy glare that expressed her true feelings.

"But Callie, that's not the point," Lynne responded. "Of course we know it's not true. But now that we don't have a contract, we need all the publicity we can get."

"I suppose you're right." Callie's response was subdued. Until her official departure, she was determined to maintain her allegiance to the group. Although she was accustomed to such publicity, it annoyed her to be linked with Tom. Still, it came with the territory. She knew she had overreacted only because of Rob.

She pushed aside her anxieties and concentrated on the session, which proved to be a therapeutic diversion. How grateful she was to have developed this professional discipline!

Callie could hear her voice blasting the upbeat melody:

> You made a fool of me, so what does that
>   make you?
> Thought you were very smart, the way you
>   broke my heart.
> It'll come back on you, someone will hurt you
>   too . . .

You made a fool of me, so what does that
  make you?
What does that make you . . .

As the song ended, her voice trailed from a dy-
namic squeal to a hushed whisper. She gazed
around the studio as if she were seeing it for the
last time.

The stage upon which she stood, cold metal microphone in hand, was elevated a few feet about
the large, long room. Devoid of video cameras
and equipment, it appeared bigger than usual.
Folding gray metal chairs were scattered ran-
domly on the scuffed linoleum floor. Vic and Greg
were sitting and talking on two of them. Gone
were the usual pack of hangers-on. The recording
crew in the glass-enclosed control room at the far
end could barely be seen behind their mounds of
equipment. A metal and Masonite table stood
against one wall. It was cluttered with empty coffee cups, filled ashtrays, soft drink cans, and a
telephone that was automatically turned off while
they were recording. Double swinging doors
dominated the other wall. Otherwise the studio
was nondescript, save the yellow ochre walls that
were badly in need of painting.

It's hard to get sentimental about such sur-
roundings, Callie reflected. And yet, that's exactly
what she was doing. Of course it was not the studio she would miss, but the years she had spent
there recording with Sizzle. Although the sessions
had often been difficult, they were usually excit-

ing, and nearly always satisfying. She knew that
her years with the group would always have a
special meaning to her. But she also realized that
it was time for her to move on.

By break time, however, her nostalgic mood became overshadowed once again by her anxiety
about Rob. She hurried to a telephone and dialed
his number. Still no answer. She called the operator, who told her that the lines were being re-
paired as quickly as possible and that they should
be in service by that evening. While she was fairly
well convinced that the reason she had been unable to reach him was the power failure, her concern was coupled with anger. She would not be
able to relax until she spoke with Rob and had the
answers to her unresolved questions.

Upon reentering the studio, Vic pulled her
aside.

"What's wrong, Callie? You look as if you lost
your best friend."

"Maybe I have." He knew her so well!

"Do you want to talk about it?"

"Sure. I'll treat you to lunch."

Of all the changes that were soon to take place
in her career, she was hoping that one thing
would remain constant—Vic. She wanted him to
be with her. He gave her the needed push when
she was down, the encouragement to continue
when she felt like quitting, not to mention the
good business and public relations advice. Besides, she reflected as they were seated in a quiet
booth at Hamburger Hamlet, he had become such
a good friend.

"Do you want the good news or the bad news first?" Callie inquired as her eyes became accustomed to the dim lighting.

"Good news! I'm always in the mood for good news."

"How would you feel about never having to go on the road again?"

"Do you even have to ask? But that's a question, not news."

"Well, the news is that you never have to! That is, you'll never have to if you take me up on the offer I'm about to make. Which leads to the bad news. I'm leaving Sizzle. It's something I have to do. And I'd like to take you with me, as my manager."

"Why, Callie—I don't understand."

"I just got a leading role on 'Trinity Bluff'!"

Vic's eyes were round with surprise. "My God! That's fantastic—I guess. I mean, well, this has really taken me by surprise. I have to congratulate you on the part, but I'm sure it's going to be a real blow to Sizzle."

"Believe me, I've thought about that a lot." Pushing away blond hair from her eyes, she sighed. "But I can't take the lifestyle anymore. I need a change. Besides, I am replaceable—the group was together long before they hired me. Chicky might do quite well, and her being with the group would make Tom a lot happier on the road. And, not to diminish your importance, but Greg would undoubtedly give his gold pinky ring to step into your shoes."

"Mmm . . ." Vic lifted his eyebrows as he pondered her statement. He took a few bites of his oversize hamburger before continuing. "You know, I had a feeling you had something up your sleeve these last few weeks, but I assumed it had to do with Rob."

At the mention of Rob's name, the excitement of telling Vic her news vanished. A queasy feeling entered her stomach, which increased as she eyed her mostly untouched platter. Her appetite seemed to have vanished.

"So what about my offer?" She intentionally changed the subject.

"Well, this is all so sudden, I don't quite know what to say."

"How about yes?"

"Whew!" Vic let out a deep breath. "You've just thrown me an offer that's hard to resist. But I'll have to think about it. It isn't something I can decide without a lot of thought. I'll let you know —soon."

Callie stared at her hamburger, noticing that the two bites she had taken formed unattached crescents in the bun. She dabbed a French fried potato in a glob of catsup, but stopped midway, placing it on her plate again. She doubted she could digest anything. The greasy aroma nearly made her gag.

"You've hardly touched your food," Vic observed. "Something's wrong, isn't it? Are you upset that I didn't jump at your offer?"

"No. No. It's not that," Callie confided. "I don't

blame you for wanting some time to think about it. I'm upset about something else."

"Well, whether I become your manager or not, I hope that I'll always remain your friend. And I hope you'll always be able to come to me with any problem you may have." Vic gave her an encouraging look. "Unless you'd rather not talk about it."

"Actually, if I don't talk about it, it'll be worse. I know that. It's Rob."

Vic raised an eyebrow.

"You see, he was supposed to meet me at the studio yesterday so we could celebrate his completing the soundtrack. I was going to tell him about the part on 'Trinity Bluff' then. But he never showed up."

Vic's eyebrows drew together, forcing his already lined forehead to crease further. "That's odd. That's very odd, indeed."

"What is?"

He remained silent for a moment, his eyes squinted in deep concentration. "Yesterday when you were out, there was a call. I'm almost sure it was for you. Tom took it. I assumed he gave you the message."

"The message . . . no. Tom never said a word to me about a phone call." But he had given her those glaring smirks, which now took on an added meaning.

Callie lunged from her seat. "I know he's behind this!"

Vic reached for her arm. "Wait a minute.

There's something else I think you should know.
Rob was due at the studio today. He's supposed to
review the final mix of 'Has Gotta Be Real' for
approval before release. He's probably there now.
Why don't you run on ahead? I'll get the check."

Callie started to dash out the door but suddenly
stopped. "But this is supposed to be my treat."

"Forget it. You'll make it up to me."

Everything blurred as she rushed toward the
studio. Shops and restaurants, pedestrians and
cars, and the crisp sunshine were obliterated by
her racing thoughts full of unanswered questions.
Why hadn't Rob stopped by that morning to see
her? Or could she have already left for lunch with
Vic and have missed him? But her intuition led
her to believe that wasn't the case. Or was she just
being paranoid? Then, was he avoiding her? And
why?

Suddenly, upon entering the lobby, she halted.
She had no idea where he might be. But she knew
that Clement McNeary, the watchful security
guard who had been with Electric far longer than
any of the other employees, would know.

"Hi, Clem . . ." Callie caught her breath as she
approached the security clearance desk.

"Hi, Callie. You look like you're in a big hurry."

"Actually, I am. I'm looking for Rob Matthews.
Do you know where he might be?"

"Well, I can't say for sure, but if you want to
catch him, you'd better hurry. He just left like a
bat out of hell and I'd say he was real mad about
something."

Oh, no! Was he angry that he hadn't been able to find her? Or was there something else? How could he leave without seeing her? Or had he tried? She didn't allow herself to meditate on these questions, but rather darted in the direction of the parking lot, hoping to reach him before it was too late.

Her eyes scanned over the rows of cars until she spotted Rob's green Jaguar. Confused but without hesitation she headed in its direction. She moved quickly toward the car. Behind the tinted windshield she could see Rob, concentrating on something. It wasn't until she got closer that she caught sight of the magazine he was staring at with an anguished look on his face. He was too involved in his own thoughts to notice her approach.

Something wasn't right. She sensed that at once, even before she knocked on the car window to get his attention. His shocked and hostile look immediately confirmed her suspicions, but when he made no attempt to get out of the car or lower the window, she knew that something was abysmally wrong.

"Rob! I need to talk to you!" She yelled the words, not knowing if he could hear her from inside the car.

Bewildered, she stood there until he finally lowered the window. He avoided her eyes as he snapped, "We have nothing to talk about."

"What do you mean, we have nothing to talk about? How can you say that after standing me up last night?"

"I stood you up? I was at the studio but you weren't. Then I went to your house and waited until nearly eleven, but you never showed up. Of course, now I know why."

"I'll tell you why—"

"Don't bother. I already know. A picture is worth a thousand words!"

He thrust the magazine in her direction. Callie was once again confronted with the picture of her and Tom.

"For God's sake, Rob! Don't tell me you believe that nonsense!"

"What I don't believe," he glared at her, his eyes icy with anger, "is how you played me for such a fool. Did you think by being coy and leading me on I would let you do anything you wanted with my songs? Especially after you led me to believe that we had come to an agreement. How could you have double-crossed me like this?"

"What are you talking about?" Callie was beside herself with disbelief.

"You know exactly what I'm talking about. I don't know what I'm angriest about—the way you stepped on me emotionally or your total disregard for my professional integrity. But let me tell you this, I'm not going to let you get away with it!"

"I . . ." Callie was too shocked to complete the sentence.

Rob continued. "You know that song you were singing this morning—'you made a fool of me, so what does that make you?' *You* answer the question—what does that make *you?*"

Callie stood transfixed as Rob rolled up his window. She still hadn't been able to open her mouth. Rob looked the other way as he revved the motor, effectively drowning out her words of wounded protest. She stood dumbfounded in the crowded parking lot as Rob deftly backed his car out and was gone.

She couldn't move from the spot. A sinking feeling overtook her. Her first thought was to race home and fling herself on her bed, but she knew she couldn't do that. She couldn't let herself fall apart. Not now. She had work to do.

Wasn't she a professional? Hadn't the morning's session helped alleviate her uncertainty? But no! A sob broke through despite her attempts to cover up her hurt feelings. Now the ambiguity was over and the reality set in—she and Rob were through. She couldn't believe it! But as she relived the scene that had just transpired between them, she knew only too well that it was true.

"My God, Callie! We've been looking all over for you. Old Clem told me you headed in this direction."

Vic's familiar voice took her out of her torturous thoughts. She became aware of herself standing transfixed in the crowded parking lot. She shook her head, realizing that she had lost track of time.

"Oh, Vic, I'm sorry! I—ah—I was just on my way back in. I'm . . ." She couldn't stop her voice from cracking.

"Callie. Callie." Vic took her into his arms. "What's the matter, Callie?"

"Oh, Vic." She sobbed as she fell into his fatherly embrace.

"There, there." Vic patted her on the back and surprisingly produced a clean handkerchief from the pocket of his leather jacket. "It's going to be all right."

"Oh, no, Vic—it isn't!" Callie wiped away tears as she blurted out her story.

"Listen, Callie—it's only a lover's quarrel. Believe me, Margaret and I have had plenty of those over the years."

His attempt to console her was useless. Callie knew from the look in Rob's eyes that it was all over.

Suddenly, a burst of strength came to her as she assured herself—*no, it's not all over. I have my career. No, I won't let myself get bent out of shape like I did with Nick. I won't let that happen again.*

"Really, Vic." She took a deep breath and attempted to force a smile. "I appreciate your listening to my personal problems, but we have work to do. I'm really sorry if I've held things up. I forgot myself."

Vic, looking worried despite her assurances, told her that she hadn't held them up—they were working on background instrumentals. "In fact, we really won't be needing you any more today. I was just concerned when you didn't show up. Why don't you take the rest of the day off. Things will look different tomorrow."

But I don't want the rest of the day off, she felt like screaming. *I want to go back to work—I want*

*to throw myself into the music and forget about
what just happened here in this lousy parking lot!*
Instead, she merely said, her voice hardly shaking
at all, "Oh, that's okay, Vic. Really, I can work
now."

"No. No. I insist, Callie. You get some rest. Call
me if you need someone to talk to, but go home
and take a hot bath or whatever it is you do when
you need to relax. You'll see, things will look better tomorrow."

Tomorrow. She sighed as she sank into the seat
of her car, her eyes still burning from her tears.
Tomorrow . . . If only she could change the way
things were going today! If only she could have
Rob and her new career. But it appeared that she
wasn't meant to have both. How ironic, she reflected, how utterly, horribly ironic.

While staring into space for several minutes,
she reflected upon the bitter argument she and
Rob had just had. How unfair of him to not allow
her to explain things! She could understand how
he could be angry about the picture in the magazine. But still, she could not comprehend what he
was talking about when he accused her of double-
crossing him. Whatever could he mean by that?

Within seconds she was racing back to the studio with the intention of finding out. She didn't
know why, but she had a feeling that the answer
lay there.

"So Lover Girl returns to the scene of the
crime," Tom announced when she entered the
room.

"Haven't you caused enough trouble already?"

"Me? What's eating you now? Don't tell me you're still mad about that picture in *Pop Star*."

"Cut it out, Tom," Vic said, trying to intervene. He pulled her aside and whispered, "I thought I told you to go home and get some rest."

Before she could respond, Tom interjected, "Well, listen, Vic, I don't know why she should be mad at me. At least I haven't refused to allow the videotape to be released like her lover boy has."

"What!"

"It's true." Tom gave her the smirk he'd been using the past few days. "Rob's panned 'Has Gotta Be Real.' "

"I don't believe it!" Callie looked at Vic for reassurance, but all she saw was a sorry look upon his face.

"I'm afraid it's true, Callie. He has final say and he's exercised his option."

"But . . . but . . . we'd agreed to a compromise."

"I know that." Vic didn't attempt to hide his exasperation. "Listen, Callie, there's nothing anyone can do about it now. Why don't you just go home and get some rest. Tom and I are going over some drum tracks for 'You Made a Fool of Me.' Everyone else has split for the day. We'll deal with the videotape tomorrow."

No wonder Vic had insisted that she go home. He was trying to protect her from becoming hurt any more than she already was.

But it wasn't hurt she was feeling now, it was anger. Talk about double-crossing! She could hardly believe that Rob could be so vindictive.

And to think he actually had the nerve to talk about "professional integrity!"

The Santa Ana may have roared intensely the night before, but its fury was nothing like the rage that was building up inside Callie Stevens.

Chapter Thirteen
❖ ❖ ❖

SHE WASN'T GOING to let herself fall apart. She couldn't allow that to happen. That's what she kept telling herself. She told that to Sharon on the phone when she refused her offer to come over. What she didn't tell her friend was that it was too painful for her to see her and her family tonight. Was she never to have that for herself?

Replacing the receiver, she felt lonelier than ever. It was like a shadow echoing throughout her empty house. She played back the messages on her answering machine, but the flashing red light had given her false hope—there were only two calls, both from Vicki requesting she come in to sign the contract for "Trinity Bluff." The excitement in Vicki's voice was so opposite to the hollowness she was feeling that it sounded abrasive as it echoed in the room. All she could think of was her loss.

But no! She stifled the sob. She wouldn't allow

herself to think about Rob. She'd concentrate on the positive, the role on "Trinity Bluff" and a new beginning. She wouldn't dwell on the past and the finale of a relationship she thought would last forever.

Despite her determination to be strong, the gnawing ache remained as tears flooded her face throughout the restless night. She couldn't wait until the morning. Surely signing her television contract would lift her spirits.

"But I don't understand. This doesn't make sense!" Callie insisted as she paced the length of Vicki's sleek office. A trail of blue smoke from her agent's cigarette drifted through the air and she waved it away. "This contract is for only thirteen weeks!"

Her voice sounded frightened. First Rob, and now this. She had assumed the contract would be for at least a year.

"Darling, believe me, there's no reason to be so upset. This is a standard contract." Vicki avoided her eyes as she squelched her cigarette in a glass ashtray on her cluttered desk and extended a slender gold pen in Callie's direction.

"How do you expect me to give up everything for what's only a thirteen-week commitment?"

"I can assure you they'll use you the entire year, but until you've been on the show for a season, this is the best anyone could do for you. I handle Mel Peters and he's been on the show for years on an optioned contract. But I'll fight for you next year—I promise you that." Vicki attempted a tight smile as she placed the gold pen on a pile of papers on her desk. She lit another slim cigarette. "I'm surprised you didn't know about the way the networks work. I mean, I can understand someone like Lauren Banks not understanding this—"

"Lauren Banks! But I thought she was up for the role of Brigette too!"

"Lauren Banks up for Brigette!" Vicki let out an incredulous laugh. "You must be kidding! Lauren got the role of Penny, a bit part on the show. There's no way they'd hire an unknown for Brigette!"

"And yet they won't give me a better contract." Callie shrugged her shoulders in resignation.

"Oh, I'm sure it's just a matter of time," Vicki attempted to reassure her as she placed her cigarette in the ashtray and once again offered the gold pen.

Callie pushed her blond hair from her face and approached Vicki's desk. As she accepted the pen she silently acknowledged that she was ready for a change regardless of the contract. She knew she was taking a big risk, but she realized that it was what she had to do. "Yeah, I had forgotten how it worked," Callie said, sighing. Scribbling her name across the line felt anticlimactic. Or perhaps that was because Rob wasn't to be a part of this new chapter in her life.

She tucked the copy into her huge leather shoulder bag and left Vicki's office. As she reached her Mercedes, squealing cries jarred her out of her private thoughts.

"Callie Stevens! It's Callie Stevens! Oh, can we have your autograph?"

She forced a smile, glancing at the group of energetic teenagers in trendy oversized shirts and skintight pants. Surprised that they weren't in school, she suddenly realized they were probably off for their winter recess. Hadn't it been only days before that she and Rob were making plans for Valentine's Day?

The autograph seekers kept babbling at a rapid speed, not allowing her to dwell on that question. She welcomed the buzzing confusion as she repeatedly signed her name for them. The beaming faces temporarily took her out of her despair.

As she waved good-bye to the well-wishers, she thought of the hectic day that lay ahead. She drove back to the studio, debating whether she should tell the group that she was leaving, but decided against telling them yet. Two more weeks wouldn't matter in finding a replacement. Besides, it was imperative that they make the best of the remaining sessions. Especially now, since Rob had vetoed the video. There was no way they could make another one. Dammit—he knew that too! How could he refuse to release the video because his feelings were hurt?

She parked her car and marched to the studio, determined not to think of Rob. If only the sun weren't shining so brightly and radiating on her partially exposed skin, making her recall other sunny days in the past. If only the sky weren't glowing so vividly blue, reminding her of Rob's deep blue eyes. The cheery weather reminded her of just how miserable she was feeling.

As she entered the studio, she breathed a sigh of relief, grateful for the dim lights and the chill in the overly air-conditioned room. Most of all, she welcomed the hectic session that would demand all her energy.

The recording went well. For the most part, she kept her mind on the music. When it ended Vic approached her. "How 'bout that raincheck for dinner tonight?"

"Oh, really, I—"

"Come on, Callie. It will do you good. Besides, Margaret is trying out a new recipe and would welcome another guinea pig."

"Oh, Vic, I don't know. I don't think I'd be very pleasant company."

"You've got to come! Margaret will be so disappointed if you don't. Besides, we have something to celebrate—our new partnership."

"My offer! You're taking me up on my offer!"

"You're right!"

"Oh, Vic, I'm so glad to hear that."

"So was Margaret. And we won't take no for an answer!"

Later that evening, as she sat in the Wilsons' dining room admiring Margaret's flourishing plants, she was glad she had been pushed into accepting the invitation.

"Now, why don't you have a second helping of that pie," Margaret insisted. "You're going to waste away to nothing."

Next to Margaret's bountiful figure, Callie realized she would appear too thin. Had she lost weight over the past few days because she had been too miserable to eat?

"I can't begin to tell you what a relief it is to me that Vic won't be going on the road anymore," Margaret declared as she plopped another piece of pecan pie onto Callie's plate. "And of course we're all so thrilled about your getting that part in 'Trinity Bluff.' It's such a great show—I haven't missed an episode since it began."

As Margaret cleared the table, Vic mentioned the unmentionable, the subject that had been lurking silently in the air. "I just don't understand what happened with the video. I thought you and Rob had reached an agreement."

"So did I." A wave of depression spread through Callie at the mention of Rob's name.

"I'm sorry. I shouldn't have brought that up," Vic uttered. "I meant for this to be strictly an enjoyable evening."

"Look, I'm going to have to get used to it." Callie knew she was telling that to herself as much as to Vic.

"I just wish there was something I could do," Vic offered. He took her hand and gave it a consoling squeeze.

"Thanks for your support, but there's really nothing anyone can do."

Vic broke the uncomfortable silence. "I don't know"—his forehead creased with concentration —"it just doesn't make any sense."

His words planted in Callie's head a thought

that grew throughout the weary weekend. Vic had seen it too, and it didn't make any sense. Hadn't she made the changes that they had agreed upon? As angry as Rob may have been about the other evening and as upset as he was about the magazine, it didn't seem possible for him to do this solely for personal reasons. Such unprofessional behavior was totally unlike him. And what about his reference to her double-crossing him? What was that all about?

Callie spent Saturday shopping in old jeans and a flannel shirt, hoping that no one would recognize her. Even adoring fans couldn't have cheered her. She went through the motions of trying on new spring fashions, but even thoughts of her great "Trinity Bluff" wardrobe couldn't dispel her gloom. Yet, it was better for her to be out among the bustling crowds of weekend shoppers than alone in her house, where she futilely longed for the telephone to ring so she could hear the sound of Rob's voice.

She couldn't stop thinking of him. She would pass a counter display for men's cologne and catch a whiff of the tangy scent he used; she would catch a glimpse of a soft wool sweater like the one he had lent her and recall the night she had returned it—the night they had shared their first embrace.

She couldn't dismiss the notion that something wasn't right. Somehow the pieces didn't fit together. The answer must lie with the videotape. That suspicion planted by Vic's words grew until she could ignore it no longer. She had to see that tape! She would just have to wait until the studio opened on Monday. Until then she would have to get through the weekend as best she could.

Time crept by torturously until Monday finally arrived. She rushed to the studio, insisting to Vic, "I've got to see that tape!"

"Okay. We've got some extra time."

He instructed Greg to take over for some back-ups and he and Callie dashed to the screening room. As soon as the tape came on, she knew something was wrong. The revised tape began with a close-up of her; this tape, like the original, showed a long shot with the band behind her. By the time the chorus came on, Callie was fuming! She was not surprised to hear the line in the chorus that Rob had objected to:

> *Has gotta be real.*
> *Has gotta be real.*
> *The way that I feel.*
> *Has gotta be real.*

It *was* the first tape—not the remake!

"I don't believe it!" Vic was shaking his head in disgust. "There's got to be an explanation! This isn't the revised tape."

"No wonder Rob refused to allow this to be released." Callie sighed, feeling more miserable than ever. "Now I know why he thinks I double-crossed him!" But, she added to herself, he could have at least given me a chance to explain.

"Well, I'm going to check into this right now," Vic insisted.

Callie had already figured it out. Someone must have taken the note she had left Rob, and that same person switched the tapes. It had to be Tom. There was no way she could prove it, but intuitively, she knew it must be true. And while the harm had already been done, she was determined at least to let Rob know what had happened. How dare he accuse her of double-crossing him!

"Vic, I need to make a quick phone call."

"Why don't you use the phone in my office. I'm sure you'd prefer some privacy."

"Thanks, Vic. But don't worry. I know how pressed we are for time. I'll keep it short."

She didn't allow herself the time to get anxious about calling him. She was too angry to let her personal feelings get in the way. The moment she heard his voice, she blurted out, "Rob, this is Callie."

"I—"

"I want you to hear me out," she commanded as she interrupted him. "I don't care if you're foolish enough to believe the stupidity printed in some libelous gossip sheet, but I *do* care that you have the nerve to doubt *my* professional integrity! And I want you to know that I had never intended for the original version of that tape to be released. The tapes have been switched, but I had nothing to do with it. You should have realized that. Vic's taking care of it now, and he will call you when he locates the revised tape. But I'm so angry, I don't think I ever want to talk to you again!"

She slammed the receiver down and took a deep breath. The nerve of him, to think that she had switched the tapes! And all this time she had believed they had been building a trusting relationship. Hah! So much for his toasts to honesty.

She forced herself to continue the session, intentionally avoiding contact with Tom. She wasn't going to allow her ill will toward him to interfere with the job that had to be done. Once she began singing, she put aside problems and poured herself into the tune, finding hope and encouragement in her art. The fulfillment of her dream of being a star was proving to be all she needed at that moment. She was actually glad that the session ran overtime. She was happy to be so involved with the music.

When Clem entered the studio, Vic announced, "We'd better call it a night. You've all done a great job, but if we don't stop now, I doubt if any of us are going to make it back here on time tomorrow."

"Yeah, we're beat," the group echoed.

As they filed out, Vic approached her. "Callie, are you going to be all right?"

"Yeah, I'm fine, Vic. Why do you ask? Was I off in the session?"

"Quite the contrary. You were stronger than ever. But I'm concerned about you. The past few months have been rough."

"That's sweet of you." Callie leaned over and planted an affectionate kiss on Vic's cheek. "But really, I'm going to be fine. Just fine."

As she headed home on Sunset Boulevard, she

vowed to make her words come true. Determined to keep her promise to herself, she impulsively pulled into a nursery, deciding to buy some plants for her home. She had been inspired by the beautiful plants in Vic and Margaret's house. Hadn't she read somewhere that caring for plants and flowers was good for your health? If she couldn't nurture a man, she'd try her hand at a ficus. Not only would her house appear more lived-in, but she'd have something to talk to at night.

Despite the long session that day, she had an abundance of energy and was determined to put it to good use. Once she had the plants arranged in the living room, it did take on a more homey appearance.

It felt good to be involved in something frivolous for a change, and as she threw herself into the task, she realized that she had forgotten about her mail and answering machine.

She had also discovered a package from Sharon beneath the mailbox. Her note said it was to celebrate getting the series part. "How thoughtful," Callie reflected as she placed the beautifully wrapped present on the couch next to a huge potted palm she'd already named Oscar.

She then pressed the playback button on her answering machine and began watering her new plants as she listened to the messages. Her mother's voice came on. "Callie sweetheart, sorry I missed you. Just wanted to give you a call and see how you are and remind you that you're welcome here anytime . . ." Callie frowned. The last time she had spent a vacation with her mother she had felt like a complete outsider. Her mother had been totally absorbed with Callie's stepfather and his children. No, she'd rather fly her mother to Los Angeles as soon as her depression lifted and spend some time with her alone.

The call was followed by a hang-up and then: "Callie. It's Rob. Please, Callie. Call me. I need to talk with you."

The spray mister opened as it fell from her hands, splashing onto the hardwood floors. As she mopped up the mess, she was determined not to return his call. What good would it do? He already had clearly shown her that he did not trust her. Standing up, she made a vow to forget about Rob and concentrate on her new career in television. Yes, maybe this was for the best, she told herself. Even as she squared her shoulders, she knew she was lying.

Chapter Fourteen
❖ ❖ ❖

THE NEXT DAY her resolve to forget Rob began to ebb. Maybe if she read the copy of "Trinity Bluff" that had arrived by messenger she would feel better.

She slipped the script from the large brown envelope but was unable to concentrate on the words. Instead of picturing Drew, her TV boy-friend, she kept seeing Rob. Every word in the script seemed to eerily echo the last few months of her life.

Callie glanced at her mantel, where she had ar-ranged some early valentines from friends and fans. Unconsciously, she had left a space for a card from Rob. Well, she could close that up, she thought ruefully. Suddenly, she remembered Sharon's gift. How she wished she could pick up the phone and call her, but they were back east visiting family.

Sharon's package was so beautifully wrapped that Callie hesitated. Surely the colorful paper and bright ribbons themselves were half the ex-citement of presents, Callie reflected. Still, when she saw what was inside, she didn't regret her im-pulsiveness. The gorgeous red silk peignoir set was exactly what she needed at that moment. Just touching the fine silk lifted her spirits. She had to get into it!

In the privacy of her bedroom she slid the deep red silk negligee over her slim body. It clung to her breasts and the slit up the side of the gown provided glimpses of her shapely leg. The neck-line plunged to a daring depth, revealing her firm breasts and creamy skin.

She stood before her mirror, taking in the im-age she projected. No longer was she a naive star-let struggling to make it. No, she was a star! A bright gleam lit up her eyes as she acknowledged her accomplishment.

Taking one last glance at her sensuous silky attire, she tied the satin ribbons of the matching robe. She drifted down the stairs to her dining room and poured herself a brandy. The amber liquid was soothing, calming her body and spirit. With snifter in hand, she drifted into the living room, and lit the fireplace. As she flicked on an old Billie Holiday album, the mellowness of the tune reached out to her. She curled up on the couch, content to relax in the comfortable scene she had created.

She considered returning her mother's call but was afraid she would ask her about Rob. She didn't want to talk about him. She didn't want to think about him. Instead, she opted to throw herself into the script. The sweet harmony of the music, brandy, and fire provided a soothing background.

She skimmed the first lines with interest, visualizing how she would recite them on the show. But when she reached a part where she and the hero kissed, it was the image of Rob that came to her. Why couldn't she banish him from her mind?

Suddenly, she heard a knock on her door. She wasn't expecting anyone, nor did she have a desire to see anyone. She just wanted to be left alone. The knock became louder. Maybe it was a Jehovah's Witness or a door-to-door salesman. She giggled when she thought of the expression on their faces when she answered the door in her skimpy negligee.

"Callie! Callie! Open the door! I've got to talk to you!"

Oh, no. It was Rob. Her heart began to pound and she felt faint. She didn't want to see him.

"I know you're in there. I'm not going away."

Reluctantly, she opened the door just slightly and called out, "Well, I don't want to see you."

But as soon as she caught sight of him, she was unable to retain the conviction in her voice. She tried to shut the door. But he stopped her.

"Callie, I heard you out. Now it's time you listen to what I have to say."

"Do I have any choice?"

"This isn't the way I wanted it to be. But you wouldn't return my call and we have things to talk about."

He pushed his way into the hallway. She backed away. In spite of his strong words, the dark circles under his eyes emphasized his pained expression. She couldn't help but be moved. So, he's been having sleepless nights too. Trying to avoid his eyes, she averted her glance.

"Callie! Please!" He reached out to touch her. She jumped away, but his eyes scanned her body. She became starkly aware of her vulnerability.

"Can I at least come in?"

"I don't see the p-point in it."

But she knew her voice faltered. She wished she hadn't put on the peignoir set. She wished she had worked late and not come home. Or had taken up her mother's offer and flown to Florida. Anything rather than having to confront Rob in person. It was one thing to be angry with him on the phone, but quite another when he was standing in front of her looking so intensely forlorn.

"Look, can I at least sit down?"

"Well . . ." She hesitated, but knew his question was rhetorical as she watched him sit down. "Okay. But don't expect me to offer you a drink."

She could hardly believe she had said such a thing. Her nerves must be getting the best of her. She chugged her remaining brandy. Why did she always get a rush of excitement when he was near? How could she hide her true feelings from him? Still, she knew she mustn't give in to his charms. She couldn't forgive him for betraying her trust.

"I don't expect anything after the way I acted. But I had to come to you to try to explain."

Callie said nothing. She looked at him and then at reflection of the fire in her empty glass.

"It looks nice in here," Rob observed as he sat down on the chair catercorner to the couch where she was sitting.

"Thanks," Callie muttered as she annoyedly became aware of Billie Holiday singing "That Old Feeling."

"Callie, I can't tell you how sorry I am. I was wrong to have doubted you."

"You don't have to tell me, because it's no use! You betrayed the trust I thought we had between us. If we don't have that, we don't have anything."

"You're right. I know that. And that's why I had to come here to explain things."

"Well, you're too late."

"Don't say that!"

"That Old Feeling." The words to the song kept

echoing in the room, mirroring all too well what was happening to her.

He didn't say anything but looked deep into her eyes. She tried to look away but found herself drawn into his steady gaze. If only that song weren't playing in the background. If only she weren't so deeply aware of how Rob's presence added to the romantic spirit of the room.

"I can't believe that you aren't feeling what I am now. It's been like this from the very start with us. There's always been magic when we're together."

"Don't try to charm me with your songwriter's lines," she choked out.

"You're right. I owe you more than that. I came here to apologize, not to win you over with clever words. I'm truly sorry about my behavior. Callie, you've got to believe me!"

"Do I?" She fidgeted with the satin bows on her robe.

"Callie, listen. You know how hurt I was after Gloria and I split up. How reluctant I was to trust again. But you'd gotten me over that."

He turned away from her and slowly walked over to the fireplace. He turned toward her again and looked down at her, his eyes pleading and his face glowing from the light of the nearby fire. Despite the weary look on his face he looked handsome, more handsome than she had recalled in her recent fantasy. But more than that, he looked like a man in love. The tune had changed, and Billie Holiday was singing something that blended into the background.

"Callie, give me a chance to explain or at least

give you some idea of what had happened and why I acted as I did." He spoke more slowly now, less urgently, but with even more seriousness as he continued. "The past doesn't always disappear as easily as we would like. It often leaves wounds that affect the present. Well, when you weren't at the studio or your house that night, doubts began to creep in."

"Damn that Tom," Callie cursed under her breath.

"Yeah, I finally figured out that he had something to do with this, but I didn't know that at the time. I should have left my message with Vic, but I had no reason yet to distrust Tom." He paused, adding, "Little did I know . . ."

The Billie Holiday record stopped and the hush intensified the seriousness of Rob's story. "Well, before I went to review the tape the next day, I met with Lance at Ma Maison. Who should be there but Gloria. She didn't hesitate to drag her current fiancé, as she called him, to my table. Even though I'm over her, seeing her bothered me. That might sound irrational, but I'm trying to level with you."

He fell silent for a few moments, and Callie studied his face intently. Yes, she understood how Rob felt, especially since he thought she had stood him up the previous evening.

He continued, his voice as low and sincere as the look in his eyes. "After that, not being in the best of spirits, I went to the studio and saw the tape. I should say the wrong tape, but I didn't know that at the time. I overreacted, I'll admit that, but I thought I had been set up—that you had been leading me on all this time to get your own way. And then Tom taunted me with that copy of *Pop Star*."

He stopped suddenly, his mouth tight with distaste. "Surely you can understand how angry I was. All I could do was grab the magazine from his slimy hands and get out of the studio before I slugged the creep."

He turned again. The only sound that could be heard was the crackling of the fire. She thought about what he had told her and had to admit to herself that he sounded sincere.

"I was still furious when you found me in the car. And now you know why." He turned to her once again and began to walk toward her.

She hadn't known about what had transpired before she confronted him at his car any more than *he* had known about Tom's betrayal.

His eyes implored her to believe him. "Callie my darling, you must forgive me for ever doubting you, for ever doubting us. I've been so afraid of getting hurt that I sabotaged what I care about most—us!"

His confession filled her with the recognition of his need for her, for it was a need that she had shared from the very beginning.

She believed that he was sincere, that he had always been sincere, and that he wanted the same thing as she. Now there could be no denying it. She moved to his outstretched arms and clung to his powerful body. As his lips came down upon hers, the feeling of elation ignited every part of her. She melted into the familiar warmth of his fiery kiss and clutched his neck as if to reassure herself that this was really happening.

She whispered into his ear, "My darling, my love. I never want us to fight again. I never want us to be apart again. I've been afraid of getting hurt, too, but I know now that we both want the same thing."

"Thank goodness you do." She clung even closer to him as he added, "I promise you that I'll never doubt you again."

"Don't. Don't ever. Because you mean more to me than anything else in the world."

Simultaneously, they drew apart. Their eyes met, once again filled with promise and love. Callie gazed at him and tenderly ran her fingertips down his face.

She saw his eyes move in the direction of the couch to her copy of the "Trinity Bluff" script. He stepped away from her and picked it up. "What's this?"

"What does it look like?"

"The part! You got the part! Callie, why didn't you tell me?"

"I meant to tell you the other night, but the wind got in the way."

Their eyes met in a meaningful understanding. "Mmm . . . that's a nice phrase—I'll have to use it in a song."

Of course it wasn't just the wind that had gotten in the way, but all that was behind them now, Callie exulted as Rob gleefully swung her in his arms. This was just as she had imagined he would react when he heard the news.

"I'm so thrilled! So happy for you!"

"For us."

"You're right. I stand corrected. You're absolutely right."

To emphasize the point, he pulled her closer to him and reclaimed her lips with his. The electricity between them was more than she could bear. She tasted the sweet familiarity of his kiss, drinking in the pleasure of his whispered moans. Sparks spread through her trembling body and her heart pounded out of control.

Taking her face in his hands, he pulled away and gazed into her eyes. She wished they could share this moment forever—the magnetic hush felt so perfect.

His fingers slid gently down her face, tenderly touching her neck as they eased their way to their destination. Deftly, he untied the satin ribbon that held her robe together. She felt it fall away from her body and became aware of her breasts rising and falling with her fevered breathing.

She was equally aware of Rob's burning eyes following the course his fingers had taken and pausing only where her chest heaved with gentle rhythmic movement. Suddenly, with a quick jerk of his head he looked away. His mood seemed to change. For an instant Callie became alarmed. She silently watched him as his eyes lit up as if he remembered something.

"I was going to wait until Valentine's Day to give this to you," he said as he looked directly into her eyes once again. "But when we're together I feel as if every day is Valentine's Day. Besides, this seems to be the day for surprises," he said as he extended to her a small package he had taken from the pocket of his jacket.

She took it in her trembling hands. The soft feel of plush velvet met her fingers as she gazed at the small jewelry box.

"Aren't you going to open it?"

"I don't know if I can. I feel so weak."

"Then allow me," Rob said, taking the present back.

As he opened the lid, she gasped when she saw the ring. It was a solitaire diamond surrounded by shimmering rubies.

"Oh, Rob . . ."

He took it from its velvet nest and held it out to her.

"It's strange"—his voice was but a whisper and his eyes were misty with love—"but in spite of all the experience I've had writing love songs, I can't find the words to express how much I love you and want you to wear this."

"You just have." There wasn't a doubt in her mind as the words escaped from her. Not a doubt.

He slipped the ring on her finger and pulled her into his arms. And when his lips came down upon hers, she could have sworn she heard the sweetest lovesong of all!

About the Author

Paula Williams's interests include painting and filmmaking, but it was after extensive traveling through such exotic lands as Iran, Israel, Thailand, Japan, and India that she began her writing career—a career that is sure to make her a leading lady of romantic fiction! Paula's grasp of contemporary life-styles is echoed through her characters, making her novels as smooth and fast-paced as life today. When she isn't writing, Paula enjoys raising her daughter, painting, and creating songs with her musician husband in their California home. Look for Paula Williams's next romance, *A Case for Love*, to be published in September by Pageant Books.

The End?

The end of a book is never really *the end* for a person who reads. He or she can always open another. And another.

Every page holds possibilities.

But millions of kids don't see them. Don't know they're there. Millions of kids can't read, or won't.

That's why there's RIF. Reading is Fundamental (RIF) is a national nonprofit program that works with thousands of community organizations to help young people discover the fun—and the importance—of reading.

RIF motivates kids so that they *want* to read. And RIF works directly with parents to help them encourage their children's reading. RIF gets books to children and children into books, so they grow up reading and become adults who can read. Adults like you.

For more information on how to start a RIF program in your neighborhood, or help your own child grow up reading, write to:

RIF
Dept. BK-1
Box 23444
Washington, D.C.
20026

Founded in 1966, RIF is a national nonprofit organization with local projects run by volunteers in every state of the union.

LOOK FOR THESE NEW TITLES
FROM PAGEANT BOOKS!

SUMMER LOVE MATCH
Marjorie McAneny

In tennis as in love, a challenging partner makes the game a thrilling match! But unlike tennis, where "love" means nothing, Jenny and Lance discover that love means everything in the real world.

ISBN: 0-517-00063-6   Price: $2.50

TO TAME A HEART
Aimée Duvall

Keeping a relationship strictly professional is tough when a handsome scientist tangles with his feisty female researcher! Together, Chris and Joshua are an equal match for stubbornness and smarts—and even more suited romantically! From the best-selling author of more than fourteen romance novels.

ISBN: 0-517-00073-3   Price: $2.50

IN PERFECT HARMONY
Elizabeth Barrett

She swore off love—and music—until a glorious new romance reawakened the song in her heart! But if their love is to·last, Nicholas must make Catherine believe that their union will bring a lifetime of shared joy and harmony. Will Catherine put her ego on the line for the love she craves?

ISBN: 0-517-00090-3   Price: $2.50

ON SALE AUGUST !